"I'm no good for you, Jessie."

He clasped her upper arms firmly. "You're a beautiful, intelligent, desirable woman, Jessie. But I don't play games—it's not my style."

"I don't, either," she said, her breath and reason threatening to desert her.

"Look, I'm warning you off in the nicest way I know how." Mitch released his hold on her, and ground out, "Trust me, sweetheart, if you're smart, you won't have anything to do with me."

Jessie had told herself the same thing only minutes before. But this wouldn't be the first time that she hadn't followed her own advice.

ABOUT THE AUTHOR

Suzanne Simmons Guntrum has traveled to forty of the fifty United States and has lived in seven, though she now makes her home in Indiana. She feels a special attraction to the Heartland, and to the women there—past and present—who have made the region what it is today. It is the lives of those women that she likes to write about. Suzanne has also long been fascinated with the Golden Raintree and has one planted in her backyard. Recently, a Golden Raintree was planted in her honor at the New Castle–Henry County Public Library, which Suzanne considers the greatest honor bestowed upon her.

Books by Suzanne Simmons Guntrum
HARLEQUIN AMERICAN ROMANCE
353–THE GOLDEN RAINTREE

SUZANNE SIMMONS GUNTRUM

HOME IN HIS ARMS

Harlequin Books

TORONTO • NEW YORK • LONDON
AMSTERDAM • PARIS • SYDNEY • HAMBURG
STOCKHOLM • ATHENS • TOKYO • MILAN

For R.R.G. forever

In memory of my grandmothers:
Louise Sessler Noeding and Jeanne Gross Simmons,
and my grandmother-in-spirit, Ida Riley

Special thanks and gratitude to the people of New
Castle and Henry County, the Historical Society, my
many friends and former neighbors, and a special
thank-you to Dr. Jeri Horn—a Friend in the truest
sense of the word.

Published November 1991

ISBN 0-373-16416-5

HOME IN HIS ARMS

Chapter One

The Long Way Home

She never forgot the first time she saw him. She never forgot the first words he said to her.

"Remember me?"

Jessie turned and looked up at the man towering over her. She automatically ran down a checklist. Jet-black hair. Eyes an unusual color: not an emerald green, but more the patina of antique jade. Muscular. Tall. Somewhere in the range of six-two or six-three. Small but distinct bump on the bridge of the nose. He'd had it broken once or twice. Scar on the jutting chin, origin unknown. Age: midthirties. Not a handsome man, at least by traditional standards, but a fascinating, even compelling, one in appearance for all that.

Jessie was quite sure she'd never seen him before. "I'm sorry, have we met?"

"You're Jessamyn Jordan, aren't you?"

She hesitated. Then, with a slight frown bracketing her mouth, replied, "Yes."

He stuck out his hand. "Mitchell Jade."

The frown disappeared. "Of course. I should have known who you were from my grandmother's description," she said as his hand engulfed hers. His grip was firm; he made no allowances for the fact she was a woman. Jessie liked that.

Dark brows arched quizzically. "Christine's description?"

Jessie nodded, and found his eyes unavoidable. "She told me you were a newspaperman, but that you looked like a boxer."

"Ex-boxer. Light heavyweight. Navy."

Jessie *didn't* like that. She had always considered boxing cruel and inhumane, and anything *but* a sport. What was sportsmanlike about two men trying to beat up each other?

Mitchell Jade rubbed the scruff of his neck and changed the subject by admitting, "We've never been properly introduced, Ms. Jordan, but somehow I feel as though we've met. Just before she became ill Christine and I spent an entire afternoon looking through the family album. There were several recent snapshots of you standing in front of an old church somewhere."

Jessie tried to recall exactly which photographs from this last trip abroad she'd mailed home to her grandmother. "Perhaps it was the Church of Trinità dei Monti," she said with perfect Italian intonation. She went on to explain, "I was in Rome earlier this spring."

"Yes. I know," he said, falling silent for a moment, evidently recalling the sequence of events. "It was an official at the American Embassy in Rome who informed us your tour group had gone off to Malta."

So *he* was the one who had seen to it that she'd been notified of the turn for the worse in her grandmother's health.

Jessie was puzzled. Why hadn't the summons come from one of her relatives, or Grandmama's lawyer, or at least an old friend of the family? Christine Brick

Warren had lived in Henry County all of her nearly ninety-two years. She knew every man, woman and child within a three-county radius. Why would she choose to rely on a stranger?

Jessie looked the man straight in the eye. "My grandmother has talked about you a great deal since I got back. But I don't seem to recall your name being mentioned in any of her letters, Mr. Jade."

The man didn't back off; he met her gaze head-on. "The name is Mitch. And I made Christine's acquaintance through a mutual friend not long after I moved to New Castle. That was back in December. She asked me to locate you because she knew I'd had plenty of firsthand experience dealing with State Department red tape and overseas embassies. I've spent the past ten years on assignment in the Philippines, then Beirut, on to China, the Eastern Bloc countries, Panama, the Middle East..."

She got the picture: He didn't stay in one place long. She supposed most foreign correspondents didn't. Good ones, anyway. And this particular one was reputed to be very good at what he did. In fact, according to Grandmama, Pulitzer Prize good.

Jessie wondered what compelled a frontline journalist to accept a temporary teaching post at the local college. Grasping the first name she could recall from his list, she asked, "Isn't it a long way from the Philippines to a small town in Indiana?"

"Halfway around the word." He folded his thickly muscled arms across his chest and smiled down at her.

The smile made all the difference. The female in Jessie suddenly found the male in him intriguing rather than threatening. It seemed Mitchell Jade could be charming when he wanted to be.

She told herself she wasn't flirting with him, that flirting was something she didn't know how to do well, and it wouldn't have worked on an experienced man like this one, anyway.

"You're not originally from this part of the country," she said. He didn't sound as though he was from Indiana. Somehow he didn't look like it, either.

"I was born and raised in a small town north of Philadelphia. I left when I was sixteen." A frown quickly came and went. "Since then I've knocked around a dozen other places."

She smiled at him this time. "That explains it."

He seemed willing to play along with her for curiosity's sake. "Explains what?"

"The accent," said Jessie neatly. "It has a touch of the Philly twang to it, but I couldn't quite place the rest of it."

His grin was engaging. "I take it you're familiar with our Philly twang?"

"I was a student at Swarthmore some years ago," she informed him.

"It couldn't have been too many years ago." There was that smile again.

What was it about this man she found so fascinating? Was it the age-old adage about opposites attracting? He should be everything that she found repugnant, and yet . . ."

"That depends on your viewpoint," she said a little breathlessly. "I was graduated from college in 1983."

"Majoring in—"

"Art history. And you?"

"Journalism."

"Of course, journalism."

Mitch seemed to realize he'd been staring at her for longer than was considered polite.

He cleared his throat and said in a conversational tone, "Christine tells me you were actually born and raised here in New Castle."

She nodded. "I left after high school, but while I was in college I'd come back and stay with my grandmother during semester breaks and summer vacations. I usually had a job in a local antique store, or one of the fast-food restaurants out on State Road 3." She gave her head a shake. "Anyway, after all these years, here I am back in my hometown."

"Yes, back in your hometown," echoed Mitchell.

"Do you shop here often?" inquired Jessie pointedly.

The century-old general store, located several miles outside the city limits, didn't seem to her like his sort of place. Perhaps it was because he was dressed in a loose-fitting safari jacket and tan slacks that would have looked more at home on the streets of Nairobi—or even Philadelphia—than they did here in the rural countryside, where the farmers still wore bib overalls and caps pulled down over their eyes, caps with John Deere or Harley or Seedco emblazoned across the crown.

Not that she herself exactly fit in, by any means. Not in the bright orange Giorgio Armani silk pantsuit she was wearing with a matching soft orange chiffon blouse.

Clothes aside, she at least had a reason to be in New Castle. But what was a man like Mitchell Jade doing in the small Indiana town?

"Actually I started coming here—" it took Jessie a moment to realize he was answering her original question "—because your grandmother got a yen for a stick of peppermint candy when I was visiting her once. That's when she told me about Popplewell's. At the time I didn't realize places like this still existed."

"Popplewell's has been here since before my grandmother was born at the turn of the century."

There was a quiet, knowing chuckle. "Christine can be coy about her age, but I had it figured pretty close. Not that she doesn't look wonderful for ninety-one—she does."

Jessie agreed.

"Your grandmother told me that she used to come here as a child." The man turned his head and let his gaze roam around the one-room country store. Between the Coca-Cola sign taped to the dust-streaked glass and the cardboard placard stating We're Open for Business, sunlight poured in through the large picture window at the front of the building. A brass-trimmed cash register, circa 1930, took up one whole end of the main counter and a gumball machine from the same era most of the other end. He motioned with one large hand; the gesture seemed to encompass the entire store and its contents. "She said she liked to spend her pocket money on licorice or horehounds or sticks of peppermint."

Mr. Popplewell, seventy if he was a day and the latest in a long line of Mr. Popplewells to run the general store, ambled out from behind the counter and said to Jessie, "Christine need any sugar along with that pint of fresh cream?"

"I didn't think to ask, Mr. Popplewell. It wouldn't hurt to take an extra five-pound bag home, though."

He nodded and went off to take care of it for her.

"Popplewell's has always reminded me of a Norman Rockwell illustration," confessed Jessie. "The wooden floorboards creaking and groaning underfoot every time you take a step. The air smelling of sawdust and linseed oil, dried herbs and those small cakes of imported soap from England. Sometimes on a rainy day in the late autumn, there's an enticing aroma of fresh popcorn in the air and the scent of tart apples and gunpowder and tobacco. Mr. Popplewell keeps a bushel barrel of unshelled walnuts in one corner by the fireplace and an empty bird cage in the other. There are dusty postcards on a wire rack over by dry goods, and a glass-topped display case filled with turquoise jewelry that some peddler from Tucson sold old Mr. Popplewell a few years back."

An eyebrow crooked. "*Old* Mr. Popplewell?"

"The current Mr. Popplewell's father. The Popplewells go back a long time in these parts. There was a trading post on this spot run by a Popplewell in the early 1800's when Henry County was being settled, or so some historians claim. There are so many memories in this place. So very many memories," said Jessie softly, putting a hand to her face.

She was surprised to find that her skin was hot to the touch, and she was suddenly feeling…different, not at all like herself. It was the strangest sensation, not unlike vertigo. She thought of telling Mitchell, of warning him, but how did one say to a virtual stranger: *I can't explain it but I feel like I'm going to faint, or pass out, or throw up all over you?*

Jessie reached out and grabbed hold of the edge of the counter to steady herself.

She was definitely feeling dizzy. And light-headed. There was a loud annoying ringing in her ears. She wanted desperately to sit down, but the nearest chair was on the other side of the store.

She tried to speak and found she had no voice. Hot, salty tears pricked the corners of her eyes. For a moment everything was swimming out of focus.

Then she spotted a man standing a few feet from her. And it was the oddest thing—Jessie couldn't believe her eyes at first—for the man was dressed in what appeared to be buckskin. He carried a long heavy rifle in his right hand and there was a backpack strapped to his broad shoulders. The wide-brimmed hat on his head was made of beaver and the hair beneath it was dark brown and formed into soft curls at his nape.

But it was the eyes that caught and held Jessie's attention. She couldn't quite make out their color; they could have been dark blue or hazel or even green. It was the expression in them that she would remember later. Much later.

There had to be a logical explanation for someone dressed in frontier garb to be in Popplewell's store, she reminded herself. There had to be a perfectly reasonable explanation for what she was seeing.

But something, some sixth sense perhaps, told Jessie that the man in buckskin had nothing to do with the local playhouse, or an historical reenactment—although those were becoming popular enough, she knew—or any of the other possibilities that came to mind. An awareness bordering on recognition niggled at her. She tried to speak, certain she knew the man from somewhere. Her lips were numb when she tried to move them. She wasn't sure if she spoke out loud or at all.

She closed her eyes for an instant and when she opened them again he was gone. Vanished. Just like that.

Jessie blinked several times in quick succession. When she was able to focus she found herself looking up into the face of Mitchell Jade.

Her mouth was desert-dry, parched. "I—I'm sorry. I didn't hear what you were saying."

There was an expression of concern on his features as he apparently reiterated, "Are you okay?"

"Yes. I think so. Why do you ask?"

"You were standing there by the counter and all of a sudden you went as white as a ghost."

Jessie took a tissue from her handbag and dabbed at the beads of perspiration on her upper lip. She felt like a fool. Still, she couldn't help but notice how badly her hands were shaking, and her fingertips were like ice. "I did?"

"Yes."

She scowled. There was more. She could hear it in his voice. "And—?"

It was Mitchell's turn to scowl. "Who's Nathaniel?"

"NATHANIEL?"

"Yes. Nathaniel."

"Are you quite sure that's what I said?"

His reply was quick and firm. "You repeated the name several times."

Her lips went thin. "I don't know who Nathaniel is. I don't believe I've ever known anyone by that name." She inhaled a deep, trembling breath and looked up at him. "Exactly what did I say?"

He weighed the answer first, then told her, "You said, 'Nathaniel? Is it thee, Nathaniel?'"

She slowly repeated the words. "'Is it thee, Nathaniel?'" A shiver raced down her spine. She shook her head. "How odd."

He was watching her intently. "How odd, indeed."

"I wonder why I said that."

Obviously the man had no answer for her.

He spoke interrogatively. "Don't you remember what happened?"

It was painful to admit that she didn't. "No."

"How do you feel now?"

Jessie took another deep breath and finished with a bland, "Okay." She released her grip on the counter and started toward the cash register.

"Let me give you a hand."

"No, thank you. I can manage on my own." Just the thought of him touching her made Jessie skittish.

He was solicitous. "Are you sure you're going to be all right?"

"Yes. I'll be fine." She opened her leather handbag again, this time taking out her wallet. "How much do I owe you, Mr. Popplewell?"

"Lemme see," he said, scratching his balding head. "For a bottle of cream, a five-pound bag of sugar and some of them tea biscuits Christine's partial to—four dollars and sixty-seven cents."

She paid the man and gathered up her purchases.

"I'll walk you to your car," Mitchell volunteered. He waited until they were outside before he inquired, "How is Christine doing?"

"Some days are better for her than others," Jessie answered truthfully. "She likes to talk about the past mostly." She took out a key and unlocked the door of her grandmother's Quaker-gray sedan that she'd been driving for the past week. Sliding behind the wheel,

Jessie deposited the grocery bag on the seat next to her. She slammed the car door shut and rolled down the window before she went on. "You see, there isn't anyone left who remembers what my grandmother was like as a child, or even as a young woman. There's no one to share those memories with her anymore. I think that's as painful for her as the knowledge that she's dying."

"Maybe you're right."

Using her hand to shade her eyes from the sun, Jessie looked up at him. "Do you have any brothers or sisters, Mr. Jade?"

"It's Mitch, and, yes, I have three younger sisters and a brother."

"I envy you. I was an only child. I don't have any siblings who shared my childhood, who can sit and reminisce about the good times and the bad times, or the things we used to do with our parents. Some memories are mine alone, and that can be very lonely. I think that's how my grandmother must be feeling—lonely and alone. When she's gone, it will be more than just the end of her life. It will be the end of all she remembers," said Jessie, her throat tightening painfully. After a minute she turned the key in the ignition. "She asked about you this morning."

Mitchell leaned over, resting his forearms on the front-door window. "What did she say?"

Jessie was surprised to find she was reluctant to tell him, but in the end she did. "She wanted to know if you'd called, or stopped by while she was napping. You haven't been to see her since I got back last week." She knew it sounded like an accusation. Maybe it was.

He straightened up and just stood there, staring out over the top of the car. One hand was shoved into his back pants pocket, the other tapped out a rhythm on the car roof. He appeared to be holding back whatever it was he was tempted to say to her.

Finally he said, "I guess I thought the two of you might like some time alone."

"I appreciate what you were trying to do, but my grandmother misses you. She wants to see you. That hasn't changed just because I'm back."

He took his hand from his pants pocket and relaxed his fist. "Tell Christine I'll be by to visit her tomorrow."

She was visibly relieved. "Thank you."

"No thanks are necessary. I genuinely like your grandmother." He took a step back from the car. "My last class of the day is over at three. I should be at the farm by three-thirty, four o'clock at the latest."

She hesitated for a fraction of a second. "Until tomorrow at four, then, Professor Jade."

"Mitch," he reminded her.

"Mitch."

Jessie tried to convince herself that she was urging him to visit the farm for her grandmother's sake, but that was only partially true. She wanted to see him again for her own sake, as well. Even though he was undoubtedly the wrong kind of man for a woman like her, said a small voice inside her head. Even though he was undoubtedly trouble with a capital T.

As Jessie drove away, leaving a trail of dust in her wake, she glanced in the rearview mirror. Mitchell Jade was standing there, tall and broad-shouldered, an enigmatic expression on his face, eyes squinting against the bright afternoon sun, hands jammed into his pockets.

The breath caught in her lungs for a moment. She had a sudden flash of insight, a premonition, a warning: This man was perfectly capable of breaking a woman's heart.

She looked back again. His lips were moving, and she could just imagine what he was muttering under his breath: "Who in the hell is Nathaniel?"

Chapter Two

Home Is Where the Heart Is

It was a perfect spring day, like sun after rain. There was a touch of warmth in the air, and the sky was so brilliantly blue that it hurt the eyes. Jessie took a pair of dark glasses from the sun visor above her head and slipped them on. There. That was better, she decided, as she drove along the country road.

She could see the local farmers had been hard at work. On either side of her was freshly turned brown earth, planted, she knew, with a crop of either corn or soybeans. If it was the former, by summer's end traveling along this stretch of 400 South would be like driving through a tunnel of lush, green foliage higher than a man's head. That's how tall the stalks of corn would grow between now and Labor Day.

The countryside was coming to life again after lying dormant through the winter. The fields were plowed and seeded in long, straight rows. The giant maples and oaks, elms and sycamores were thick with new growth. Flowers grew wild alongside the fences, and here and there were clumps of sweet-smelling lilacs: bishop's purple, pristine white and palest lavender.

Jessie drove slowly, taking in deep satisfying breaths of fresh air. She stopped the car on the crest of a small rise and got out and stood looking off toward the horizon.

There was not another human being in sight. Not a building, nor a car, nor a billboard. Not even a telephone pole to tell her that she was in the twentieth century. The only sounds were the wind as it rustled through the treetops, the buzz of insects in the field nearby, the faraway lowing of a herd of dairy cows. And there in the distance was the Happy Valley. When she made the turn, she would be able to see the Brick family farmhouse and the cluster of barns and sheds that surrounded it, typical of rural Indiana.

The title of the famous song came to mind: "Back Home Again in Indiana."

A sense of belonging—strong and unexpected and bittersweet—overcame Jessie, threatening to bring tears to her eyes. This *was* her home. For such a very long time she hadn't known where home was.

She had left this place once and traveled to all the exotic lands of her dreams. It wasn't until years later that she'd walked off a jumbo jet from Singapore and said aloud, not caring who heard her or what they thought of her if they did, "Lord, it feels good to be back in Indiana!"

That was the first indication that she'd changed. There were many more. This past year was the deciding one. She had become thoroughly disenchanted with life in the city—New York took its own kind of toll on the human spirit. She had grown weary of the fast track, the hectic, stressful business of being the chief buyer and part owner of one of 57th Street's most upscale and *très chic* antique shops.

She was already anxious to return home to Indiana when the official notice of her grandmother's illness

reached her on Malta: she'd sworn it was the last time
she would escort the rich and famous on an antique-
buying junket, anyway.

She had seen enough of distant lands and towering
cathedrals and architectural wonders to last her a lifetime; too much of poverty, disease and human despair.
Years ago she had gone off in search of something.
Somewhere along the way she'd forgotten just what it
was.

What was it she'd been searching for, Jessie asked
herself as she gazed out across the green valley, the one
her family had long called the Happy Valley.

Was it something as simple as serenity?

There was a sense of the serene about this place. Perhaps it was a mistake to think that you couldn't go
home again. Perhaps she should have come home a long
time ago.

Regrets: she'd vowed that she wouldn't have any. Or
at least if she did, she wouldn't waste precious time
dwelling on them. Now was no time to start.

It was time, however, to get back home, Jessie reminded herself. Grandmama would be waiting for her.

JESSIE PARKED on the gravel drive beside the house and,
clutching the grocery sack, ran up the steps into the
kitchen. Esther Huckelby was standing at the sink preparing vegetables for their dinner.

Some seven years ago, her grandmother had made the
mistake of venturing out on a cold January morning
and had fallen on the ice-glazed steps of the back stoop.
The result was a fractured ankle and Esther Huckelby.

Esther had come "to do" for the injured "Quaker
lady" until she was back on her feet. But by spring, the
woman was a permanent member of the household. She

did everything from washing and ironing the sheers during the annual fall cleaning, to brushing Christine's hair once she was forbidden by the cardiologist to raise her arms above her head. In short, Esther had made herself indispensable.

"That you, Jessie?" the housekeeper called.

"Yes." She dropped her handbag onto the nearest chair and proceeded to unpack the few items she'd purchased at Popplewell's. "Hmm, something smells delicious," she said, sniffing the air.

"Baked Christine's favorite for dessert—banana cream pie with graham cracker crust." Esther picked up another carrot and began peeling it before she added, "Now don't you go moaning and groaning about how much weight you're gonna gain eating my home cooking. Wouldn't hurt you none to put on a few pounds. I swear you're skinny as a rail."

Jessie bit back a smile. "In Europe, this is considered fashionably slender, you know."

"Well, you aren't in Europe now. You're back in the U. S. of A., and here we call it skinny."

She decided to concede the point. "I didn't know if we needed sugar or not. I bought an extra bag at Popplewell's."

"Won't go to waste in this house. Never did see such a one for sweets as your grandma. Claims she was born with the sweet tooth and can't do nothing about it now."

"I suppose she's right," Jessie said, setting the bottle of cream in the refrigerator. "How's Grandmama doing, anyway? Is she awake?"

Esther Huckelby shook her head. "Dropped off about a half hour ago. She was looking at a picture album and plumb wore herself out, poor thing." She dried her hands on the dish towel wrapped around her ample waist, then glanced at her wristwatch. "It's time one of us checked on her. You want to go, or should I?"

"I'll go."

Jessie made her way quietly down the hall toward the large bedroom at the back of the house. The grandfather clock in the front parlor was sounding the quarter hour.

After she'd broken her ankle on the ice that fateful January morning, Christine Warren's one concession to her age and deteriorating health had been the moving of her bedroom furniture from the second story to the first. She had been downstairs ever since, although she still referred to the room in which she'd slept for the past seven years as "Mama and Papa's."

The door was standing wide open. Without making a sound, Jessie stepped into the room and walked around the end of the bed. She took a seat and waited.

Her grandmother appeared to be resting quietly. She looked even more fragile in repose, Jessie noticed, than when she was awake. Grandmama had always been a slender woman and slight of stature, but the advancing years had taken their toll. She seemed so small in the big bed, scarcely more than a bump or two beneath the quilt the housekeeper had covered her with at nap time.

The quilt was Grandmama's personal favorite, a family heirloom sewn by her grandmother, Mary Long Sutter. Mary had embroidered the date, 1868, her full name and a replica of the farmhouse, much as it was to be found then and now, into the center of the pattern. The remainder of the family album quilt consisted of colorful fruits and flowers, an elegant teapot, a horse and rider, two small handprints, gaily beribboned baskets and several majestic trees.

It was a work of art and a genuine historic treasure, as Jessie had told her grandmother numerous times over the years. She'd occasionally considered the small fortune she could get for the perfectly preserved antique quilt if it were for sale in her 57th Street shop. Not that she would ever dream of selling the quilt. She wouldn't. Under any circumstances.

"How long have you been waiting for me to wake up?" came a whisper from the bed.

Jessie looked over at the small woman and smiled. "Actually I was sitting here admiring the intricate stitching on the quilt your grandmother made."

Christine ran her bony fingers across the material in a loving caress. "In her day, Grandmother was considered an artist with a needle and thread." She let her eyes close for a moment as if she were catching her breath.

Jessie reached for the slender wrist. Sometimes she needed to reassure herself that there was still a regular pulse beating, and blood pumping through the tired old arteries. "You mustn't let on that I've told you, but Esther has made a surprise for your supper."

The older woman's eyes blinked open. Interest and curiosity shone in their pure blue depths. "A surprise?"

Jessie nodded. "Promise not to tell?"

"Of course."

She deliberately came closer and lowered her voice. "She's baked you a banana cream pie."

Christine's head came off the pillow an inch or two. "With graham cracker crust?"

"With graham cracker crust," she verified.

"Dessert always was my downfall." Christine sighed. "I never could resist the temptation of anything sweet. James used to say to me, 'sweets for my sweet.'" At the mention of her deceased husband's name she fell silent for a minute. Then, "Did you go over to Popplewell's this afternoon?"

"Yes." Should she tell her, Jessie wondered. "I ran into a friend of yours while I was there. A man named Mitchell Jade."

An expression of pure pleasure crossed Christine Warren's face. "So, you've finally met Mitchell. What did you think of him?"

"He was nice." She could tell that wasn't going to be nearly enough for her grandmother and went on. "I only spoke with him for a few minutes, but he seemed like an intelligent man. Strong. Confident, Masculine. Attractive, in a different sort of way. He said to tell you he was planning to stop by for a visit tomorrow."

"That pleases me very much," her grandmother admitted, now deeply interested. "Mitchell Jade is a favorite visitor of mine, as you may have guessed."

"I rather thought you liked him."

"You like him, too, don't you?"

She patted the wrinkled hand reassuringly. "Yes, I do." Then, driven by some compulsion she wasn't sure she understood, Jessie said, "May I ask you a question?"

Christine Brick Warren turned her face toward the young woman sitting in the chair beside her bed. "Of course you can, my dear."

She took a deep, sustaining breath. "Who is Nathaniel?"

There was a heartbeat of silence. "Nathaniel?"

"Do you know anyone by that name?"

"No—" Christine Warren's voice thinned out "—at least I don't think so. Should I?"

Jessie sighed and decided this wasn't the time to tell Grandmama about the incident at Popplewell's. "No. Not really. I just thought perhaps you might."

The old woman turned her head on the pillow and stared out the window of what had once been her parents' bedroom. "I remember so many names now, see so many familiar faces that I haven't seen or thought of in years. Just this afternoon I was dreaming about James and the War."

She knew her grandmother was often thinking these days about her husband, Jessie's own dear grandfather, who had died nearly ten years ago.

"You were in France during the First World War, weren't you, Grandmama?"

"Yes, indeed, I was."

"And Grandfather, too?"

She nodded her head; the once beautiful golden hair had turned to a shimmer of pure silver. "James served in the awful trenches on the Western Front." She turned back to Jessie and said, "Sometimes things that happened seventy or eighty years ago seem clearer to me than the events of last week." There was a hint of a self-deprecating smile. "I suppose that's a sign that I'm getting older."

Jessie leaned closer. "Not you, Grandmama. Never you."

The afternoon sun slanted in the bedroom window, bathing the room in its brilliant light: the large bed with its century-old coverlet and the starkly plain yet beautiful furniture Jessie had always associated with her grandmother. She knew it had been handed down from generation to generation through the women of her family and would, one day, be hers. She fervently hoped and prayed that day was still far away. The sheer curtains at the windows gently billowed as a soft spring breeze slipped in between the window frame and the sill.

Jessie moved her chair to one side so the sunlight wasn't shining directly into her eyes. "Would you like me to draw the shade?"

Christine shook her head. "You could fluff my pillows a little, though, if you wouldn't mind?" She sat up straighter and folded her hands in front of her while Jessie reached behind her to plump the feather-filled ticking.

"How's that?" she asked.

"Fine. Thank you, my dear."

She sat down again. "About Mitchell Jade..."

Her grandmother looked thoughtful for a moment, then seemed to make up her mind about something that had been eluding her. She said, "I believe part of the reason I like Mitchell so much is because he reminds me of your grandfather. James had that same tall, broadshouldered build, and a slightly crooked nose that had been broken several times. Only James injured his during football practice his first year of college, and I believe Mitch said his nose was broken as the result of a boxing match." A brief pause, then, "He's even promised to take me on a picnic once I'm feeling a little better."

"Who has?"

"Mitch. We're going to go on a perfect day in the middle of the summer. I remember another summer day," murmured Christine, a ghost of a smile spreading across her face. "It was July of 1917. Just before Charlie and James went off to war."

Jessie felt her scalp begin to tingle. "That would have been my Great-uncle Charlie."

"Yes. He was a volunteer driver for the Friends' Ambulance Unit." The blue eyes became dreamy, as they often did when Christine was reminiscing. "But on this one particular day when we were still all together, we took a picnic lunch and drove over to No Name Creek. There were five of us."

"Tell me more about that day, about your picnic," urged Jessie thoughtfully.

Her grandmother was agreeable. "We spread old quilts out on the grassy banks and sat and watched the dappled sunlight on the water and the weeping willows dipping into the shallow creek. Your grandfather gathered a handful of blue flowers and gave them to me. It's one of those scenes that seems permanently imprinted on my mind. Even now I can see everything and everyone exactly as they were that day." She closed her eyes and brushed her hand across the sky-blue flowers embroidered on the quilt covering her. "Forget-me-nots. Did you know they represent loving remembrance and friendship?"

"No, I didn't."

Her eyes opened. She seemed to be focusing on something in the distance. "Blue flowers were growing in wild profusion along the stream bank the day of our picnic. We were all so happy and carefree in those last few precious weeks before the war." Christine's voice thinned out again. "It changed everything."

"World War I?"

"The Great War. That's what we all called it. Even a Quaker family like ours was touched by its ruthless cruelty. It was so senseless."

Without enthusiasm, Jessie said, "War usually is."

Christine reverted to a happier subject. "James brought his badminton equipment with him and we played until I *finally* won a game. I remember the pins came out of my hair. It never would stay in place, my hair.''

"It was beautiful," murmured Jessie, picturing her grandmother's thick tresses as they had once been: long, golden-blond in color, and flowing down well past her waist. During the day, Grandmama would wear her hair neatly plaited and then coiled around her head like a coronet. But at night she would take it down and brush it, and the little girl, Jessie, would sit on the bed, transfixed, and watch her in the mirror. Now Christine's hair was cut short for expediency's sake and formed a silver cap that framed her face. Her grandmother's one great vanity, gone. It made Jessie sad to think of it.

"Some were very keen on bird-watching, I recall. My sister was going on and on about women getting the vote. And I—I wandered off by myself until James came looking for me." Christine came back to the present, clicking her tongue and scolding herself, "Now I sound like an old lady, boring you with all this talk of people you don't remember or never knew, and of times long gone."

Jessie gave her grandmother's hand an affectionate squeeze. "You're not boring me. You never have and you never will. I like it when you share the past with me."

"You do understand, Jessie. You always did." A sigh escaped her lips. "It's just that lately the past isn't very far away for me."

"Nor for me," said Jessie meaningfully, thinking of what had transpired in Popplewell's store. Then she brightened. "What did you have to eat at your picnic that day?"

Christine considered the question for a minute. "Fried chicken and fresh baked bread. Cherry pie and peach pie made from preserves we'd put up the summer before. Some of Mama's prize pickles and special corn relish. Lemonade and iced tea."

"You must have had a lovely afternoon."

"It's one of those special memories I'll always cherish. I have never forgotten that day." She patted the perfectly manicured hand beside her own and said matter-of-factly, "But enough about the past. Your birthday is this summer."

"Yes."

"You'll be thirty years old." She looked long at her granddaughter. "Will you stay?"

"I want to stay—if you'll have me."

"This has always been your home," Christine pointed out.

"I know that now," said Jessie, struggling to keep her voice even. "I do love this place." She ran one hand along the polished antique wood of the bedside table. "I love this house and everything and everyone in it."

"It's time, then." The older woman's voice came out small, but firm.

She was curious. "Time for what?"

"Time to pass on all of this." Christine made a gesture that seemed to include her bedroom, the farmhouse, the great Golden Raintree atop the hill, the family cemetery, the land and the valley beyond. "Everyone else in the family has been given their share of the inheritance. This will be yours."

She looked into her grandmother's piercing blue eyes. "Have you been waiting for me?"

"Oh, yes, I've been waiting for you, Jessamyn."

"You never said anything to me on my visits to Indiana."

"I couldn't force you to come back to stay, to carry on where I will leave off."

"Grandmama—" Her voice cracked with emotion.

"We have to face facts, my child. I'm nearly ninety-two years old. I've had a long and full life with few regrets. How many people can say that?"

Jessie wasn't sure she wanted to be having this particular conversation with her grandmother. "Not many, I suppose."

Christine gave a decisive nod of her head. "I've been more fortunate than most. I married the one man I loved and had four wonderful children with him. I've been to every place I wanted to go and seen just about everything I wanted to see. I enjoyed good health until recently, but I can tell my body is wearing out. And I do dislike malingerers. I only want a few weeks, perhaps a month or two, with you. That's what I've prayed for." She put her head back on the pillows and closed her eyes. "Strange, but I'm suddenly feeling quite weary."

Jessie could see the gray lines of fatigue sharply drawn on her grandmother's features. "Little wonder," she said with forced cheerfulness. "All this talking would be enough to tire anyone."

"I want to talk with you. I have so much I must tell you," Christine mumbled, without opening her eyes.

"There'll be other times," Jessie assured her.

"I believe I'll rest until supper. Why don't you go make yourself a cup of tea?" Christine added in a voice that was scarcely audible.

"All right. I think I will." She stood up, bent over the large bed and placed a kiss on the pale cheek. "I'll see you for dinner."

She was almost out the door when she heard her name. "Jessie?"

Turning around, "Yes?"

The blue eyes were open, and troubled. "I wish I could remember who Nathaniel was. I feel as if I should know."

"Don't worry about it, Grandmama. Rest now."

Her eyes drifted shut again. "It's good to have you home, my dear."

As she closed the bedroom door, Jessie murmured, "It's good to be home."

Chapter Three

There's No Place Like Home

"May I offer you a lift home?"

Mitchell shook his head and responded politely to the older man walking alongside him. "Thanks, anyway, Professor, but I finally broke down and bought myself a car last night."

Richard R. Ratcliff raised both distinguished-looking, slate-gray eyebrows in a questioning arch. "Bought? Not rented?"

The young journalist grinned, showing two rows of strong straight white teeth. "Bought. With cold hard cash." He switched his briefcase to the other hand and dug the keys out of his pocket. "I've imposed on your generosity and your willingness to chauffeur me around long enough. It's time I had my own 'set of wheels,' as my students would say."

There was an unmistakable element of hope in Professor Ratcliff's voice as he inquired, "Does this mean you've decided to accept the university's offer?"

Mitch furrowed his forehead in thought. "I haven't decided yet. I'm tempted, of course. The terms of the contract and the salary are generous, and the prospect of returning for the next academic year does appeal to me."

"But you're just not sure."

He had to be honest with the man who had befriended him from his first day on campus. "But I'm just not sure."

The older man reached out and patted him on the back of one broad shoulder. It was a gesture that implied he understood. "I know it's not an easy decision for you, Mitch. You've spent your entire adult life moving from place to place, chasing the next big story, living on the edge."

"And out of a suitcase," he interjected.

Professor Ratcliff nodded and went on. "Still, it must be difficult for you to consider settling down and teaching others what you might prefer to be doing yourself."

Mitchell sighed. "After my last assignment, I swore I'd never go overseas again. I was totally burned out. I never wanted to report on another ousted political leader, run through another airport to catch yet another plane, eat one more dish of food from unknown origins, or sleep even one more night in a strange hotel room. Now I'm not so sure."

How could he explain the excitement, the rush of adrenaline, the nearly addictive stimulation of being a journalist always out there on the cutting edge to someone who had never experienced it?

Now, thanks to his editor and longtime friend, he was back in the States on a teaching sabbatical. But could he settle down now and live a normal life? A life that might include a home, a wife and children, a regular job? Always knowing where he was and what bed he was sleeping in when he awoke each morning?

Or was it too late for him? Had he already passed the point of no return? Was he doomed, by his own design and desires, to spend his life searching for the next big story?

Richard Ratcliff said with candor: "It would be considered a real coup for the university if you were to accept our offer. It's not every day they can claim a Pulitzer prizewinner as a member of the faculty." His eyes rested thoughtfully on Mitch. "They won't need an answer from you until midsummer, if that's any help."

He was duly grateful. "It is."

The older man stopped and looked around the college campus with its ivy-covered stone buildings, rolling green lawns and vast natural canopy of trees overhead. "I've taught journalism at this university for the past thirty years. And I've lived in this part of Indiana all of my life. It may not be exciting or cosmopolitan by some standards, but it's home to me."

"Home," echoed Mitchell as he gazed at the tranquil setting surrounding them.

He was still thinking of what his friend and colleague had said as he climbed behind the wheel of his new car a few minutes later.

Home.

Such a plain, simple word to have so many meanings for so many people.

Home.

He had avoided thinking about his parents and the small dilapidated house on West Berry Street for years. He'd made a concerted effort *not* to think about them, in fact.

What came to mind when he thought of *home* now? Mitchell decided to pin himself down on the subject as he headed in the direction of New Castle and the Brick farm.

Home.

His eyes grew narrow and hard as bitter memories floated to the surface.

Not enough money. *Never* enough money.

Clutter everywhere and not a moment's peace.

Noise. Inside the too-small house and, worse yet, outside on the neighborhood streets.

Too damned many people.

Too many mouths to feed. Too many crying babies and screaming mothers and hard-drinking fathers. Too little love. Too much poverty and hate, resentment and violence.

The memories grew more specific. For an instant Mitchell thought he could detect the lingering odor of corned beef and cooked cabbage from the house next door to theirs, the stench of rotting garbage emanating from the alley behind the row houses. The air inside the brand new automobile suddenly seemed stale. He could almost smell the ashtrays overflowing with cigarette butts and the empty beer cans left from the night before.

Worse, he could vividly recall the shrill, angry voices of his mother and father heaping abuse on each other—and, inevitably, invariably, on their children, on him—as if it were yesterday.

What was it Jessamyn Jordan had said to him yesterday? That she didn't have any brothers or sisters who'd shared her childhood, who could sit and reminisce about the good times and the bad times, or the things they used to do with their parents. Some memories were hers alone, and that could be very lonely.

"There are worse things than being alone and lonely, Ms. Jordan," Mitchell muttered under his breath as he turned onto the country road that would take him to the Brick family farm in time for tea.

ESTHER HUCKELBY TOOK the kettle off the back burner of the stove and poured the steaming water into the ceramic teapot on the kitchen counter. "Becky Sue Stoots from down the road rang up a bit ago while you was in sitting with your grandma. Said her husband, Lyman, is coming over on Friday to plow the garden with that old Rototiller of his."

Jessie's head came up. "I'm surprised you want to be bothered with a garden this year."

"Humph. Wasn't my idea," muttered Esther. "Christine insisted. Matter of fact, as soon as she spotted the first robin this spring, she called me into the study and sat me down and said we had to figure out what we were going to plant and where. So many rows of onions, she told me, and so many rows of radishes and how many hills of them beans she's partial to did I think we should plant and so on."

Jessie smiled in understanding. Grandmama always had to have her beans.

"Then one day, a couple of weeks ago," said Esther matter-of-factly, "she was feeling real poorly so I was reading to her from the third chapter of Ecclesiastes, all about there being a time to plant, and a time to pluck up what's planted, and I mentioned something about not having a garden this year, seeing as how she wasn't herself, and Christine let me know in no uncertain terms she expected the tilling and the planting and the hoeing and the weeding to go on as it had every spring for as long as she could remember, come what may." She placed a plate of homemade cookies on the tea tray in front of Jessie. "So Lyman Stoots is acoming over at the end of the week to do the tilling," she repeated, shaking her head and clucking her tongue.

"Perhaps my grandmother wants to know, needs to know, that the garden will be there at the end of the summer—" Jessie's heart sank a little "—even if she isn't."

Esther Huckelby settled down in the chair opposite her. "Suppose you're right. Anyway, I'm not about to be the one to begrudge Christine her garden. If a garden is what she wants, then a garden is what she gets."

Jessie was sympathetic. "I know it's a lot of work for you, but my grandmother has always loved her garden."

"The work don't matter. Hard work never hurt nobody. 'Sides, none of us Huckelbys have ever forgotten that it was your family who was there with a kind word and a pie or a cake baked special for us when our mama passed on. Nobody else bothered to lend a neighborly hand. We weren't blind or dumb. We knew how folks felt about our mama. But she was still our mama. Christine understood that." Esther fussed with the cream and sugar for a minute. "Your grandma is near a saint as a body can be. Told her that to her face once. Should have seen her. Turned fifty shades of pink, she did. It embarrassed her. Her being a Quaker lady and all."

"I think it was probably more because she's Christine than because she's a Quaker," suggested Jessie.

"Either way, she don't hold with that kind of fussing. Goes about her business in a quiet way, she does. I couldn't begin to tell you the names of all the people she's helped in the years since I been in this house." Esther imparted the information as if she were privy to a good many of Christine Warren's secrets and would share them with Jessie because she was, after all, family, too.

Jessie sighed. "There aren't many women like my grandmother."

The housekeeper nodded her agreement. "Won't see her like again in my lifetime, I can guarantee you that." It was declared with an equal mixture of pride and affection.

"You've been a good friend to us both." Jessie reached across the table to touch the other woman's arm. "Grandmama couldn't have stayed in her own home the past few years if you hadn't come to help out. And when I was halfway around the world, it was a source of great comfort to me to know that you were here with her. I can never repay you for all you've done."

"Never you mind now, girl. There's nothing to repay. Your grandma ain't no bother like a lot of old folks. Even when she was laid up with that broke ankle of hers and had a right to be grumbling and growling, she always had a smile and a kind word for me." Esther's voice softened. "Nobody ever treated me as good as you two." Embarrassed at the uncharacteristic show of emotion, she straightened her back and announced, "It's time for Christine's afternoon tea."

"Speaking of which," Jessie said, pushing her chair away from the table and getting to her feet, "I expect our guest will be here any minute."

"That Mitchell Jade coming for tea, is he?"

"Yes."

Esther grunted noncommittally. "Big man."

Jessie bit a smile from the corners of her mouth. "Yes, he is."

"Seen his share of hard times, I'd venture to say."

Jessie was curious. "Do you think so?"

An emphatic nod or two of the head. "You can always tell the ones who've had to fight for every scrap they got. There's something about them. Something in the eyes."

Just as she was about to ask Esther Huckelby to explain what that something was, the timer on the oven buzzed.

"Thought I heard a car in the driveway. You run along now, Jessie girl, and let the man in while I check on the honey cake."

Jessie nodded and walked down the hall to the living room. In many ways the room was still very much the formal parlor it had been in Grandmama's youth. The furniture was stiff and uncomfortable; it wasn't meant to be anything else. The knickknacks were to be seen but not touched—after being passed from generation to generation for over two hundred years most of them were rather valuable antiques. The room was dusted and swept by the housekeeper every other day. Nevertheless, there was a general air of disuse about it.

Scooting to the front window, Jessie parted the lace curtains a fraction of an inch and watched as a small sleek cherry-red sports car pulled up in front of the farmhouse. It stopped, the door on the driver's side opened and Mitchell Jade got out.

The sudden tightening of her neck muscles, the tension in her silk-clad shoulders, the tilted angle to her head, the increasingly rapid pace of her breathing, all alerted Jessie to her obvious interest in the man.

The late-April sun picked up the highlights in Mitchell Jade's hair and turned it a beautiful blue-black. He reminded her of a large, powerful, wild stallion, not unlike one she'd seen in a movie a few years ago. The wind tousled a strand of his hair back and forth across

his forehead. His strong features stood out in relief in
the clear spring air: the once-broken nose was interesting rather than ugly, the chin was hard and uncompro-
mising, the eyebrows were two emphatic slashes above
dark-tinted aviator glasses.

He was wearing a black leather blazer over a white
dress shirt, and a pair of faded jeans that clung to his
muscular thighs like a second skin. On his feet were a
pair of scuffed loafers, no socks.

Jessie watched in silence as the man gave the car door
a nudge. It slammed shut. He carefully ran his hand
along the shiny surface of the hood, whistling under his
breath as he took a clean handkerchief from his pocket
and wiped away what appeared to be a speck of dust.
He took a step back and admired his handiwork.

Then he casually tossed his car keys into the air,
caught them again and eased them into the front right
pocket of his jeans. The material stretched tautly across
his lower body and did little to disguise the outline of his
key chain, or anything else, for that matter.

Jessie swallowed hard and reminded herself several
times that she was an adult, not a teenager with over-
active hormones. She was a sophisticated, worldly New
Yorker who had seen and done just about everything
there was to see and do—on the right side of the law,
anyway.

Still, for a few electrifying moments she forgot everything and everyone but the man coming toward the
house. How odd...she didn't remember him being so
tall.

Mitchell Jade strolled across the drive and up the
short walk. He slipped his dark glasses off, hooked
them into the pocket of his leather jacket and pro-

ceeded up the front steps. Dropping the lace curtains back into place, Jessie went to answer the door.

FOR A MOMENT Mitch stood there, staring at her.

She took his breath away, and, damn, he hadn't expected that.

It wasn't just the mass of chestnut-brown hair that brushed back and forth across her shoulders with each tiny, imperceptible movement of her head, tempting a man to bury his hands, his face, his mouth, in the silky stuff.

It wasn't the flawless complexion that required no makeup, or the elegant hands, or the long graceful body that moved like a ballerina's. It wasn't even the sherry-colored eyes—although he swore he'd never seen that distinctive shade of brown in a pair of human eyes before. Well, maybe a long time ago, but he couldn't have said where or when....

It wasn't her intelligence, although she was obviously very bright, and he readily admitted to a deep-seated aversion for stupidity in any way, shape or form, on the part of anyone, man or woman.

And it wasn't the fact that Jessamyn Jordan was "class" personified; she was obviously a lady right down to the tips of her expensive Italian leather pumps.

It was all of these things, and it was none of them, Mitch decided, that made Jessie attractive.

More than attractive. Beautiful. Irresistible. Enticing. Sexy as hell.

He nearly slipped his dark glasses back on so the woman answering the door wouldn't see what was clearly revealed in his eyes. Then he decided it wouldn't hurt for her to know up front that he wanted her.

Whether he got her was another matter altogether.

"Hello, Mitch." Her voice flowed around him like sweet, thick molasses.

He gave his jeans an unnecessary brushing with the flat of his hand. He gave her a nod and a succinct, "Jessie."

"You're just in time for tea and cake."

Tea. He didn't really drink the stuff, but his stomach began to growl at the very mention of the word cake. He'd worked straight through the lunch hour grading his students' analyses of the latest crisis in the Middle East, and he was famished.

She pressed her back against the open door and let him pass. "Esther has been baking up a storm all day."

No need to tell him. He could detect the evidence of that for himself, wafting from the back of the farmhouse. His stomach growled even louder and his mouth began to water.

This was what home was supposed to smell like, Mitch thought as he stepped into the front hall: warm and welcoming, the aroma of fresh-baked cake in the air.

The house was quiet, only the mellifluous chiming of a grandfather clock in the front parlor broke the silence. Light streamed in through lace-curtained windows, bathing the rooms facing the southern sun in rich golden hues.

He recalled in detail his first visit to the Brick family farm. It had been some months ago on a frigid December day, a day filled with snow-gray skies and the promised bleakness of a long midwestern winter.

Richard Ratcliff had insisted that Mitch accompany him as he stopped to pay his respects to an old friend, explaining, "I've known her since I was a boy. In fact, I wouldn't be the man I am today without her. She's a

very special woman, Mitch. A Friend in the truest sense
of the word.''

That Friend, of course, had been Christine Brick
Warren.

From the moment he'd stepped inside the front door
of the farmhouse, Mitch had recognized that this was a
special place, a place of peace and serenity, a haven, a
home. It was as different from the home he'd grown up
in, the home he'd run away from at the age of sixteen,
as a home could be.

He remembered Christine telling him a little of its
history. ''My great-grandparents, Elizabeth and Joshua
Banks, founded this homestead in 1821, after migrat-
ing west along the Cumberland Road from North Carolina. It's what hundreds, thousands, of Quakers did in
those days, when the issue of slavery could no longer be
tolerated. Joshua Banks, the gentleman farmer, and his
elegant wife, Elizabeth, in a Conestoga...'' Christine
had shaken her head in dismay and wonderment. ''By
some miracle they survived, cleared the land that became this farm, and built a cabin where the old red barn
sits today. The original log cabin is long gone, of course,
along with the apple orchard purported to have been
planted by John Chapman.''

''Johnny Appleseed?'' Mitch had repeated with a
questioning arch to his brow.

Christine had smiled. ''Yes, Johnny Appleseed. I
understand Elizabeth Banks cooked up more than one
kettle of rabbit stew for the wandering preacher.''

Mitch had shaken his head in disbelief.

She'd laughed quietly. ''The Bankses and the Bricks
and we, their descendants, have lived on this land for
nearly two centuries. It has been handed down from

generation to generation through the women of my family.''

A bit unusual, Mitch had thought at the time, until he learned that the Society of Friends, the Quakers, believed in equality for all men, and between men and women. It had been a solemn tradition from their founding in England over three hundred years before.

"I get a special feeling when I come here," Mitch had confided to her after he'd been visiting the farm on a weekly basis for some months. "There's something about this place..." He'd honestly not known how to describe it.

Christine had slipped her small slender hand into his and said, "I've always felt the same way, Mitch. It's the reason I moved back here after my dear James died."

"What do you think it is?" He'd wanted to know; he'd *needed* to know.

"Perhaps something as simple as love. This house has always been filled with love," she had said to him then.

Simplicity. Peace. Serenity. Love. The principles upon which the Society of Friends had been founded. Alien concepts surely, Mitch thought with an ironic smile, for a journalist who had spent his life covering the complexities of modern life, the horrors of man's ugly little wars, the inhumanity of humanity and its seemingly never-ending capacity for hate.

"What I love about my family's home—" Jessie captured his attention again and forced him back into the present "—is the fact that it never changes. Everything else, perhaps, but never this place."

"You're damned lucky," he declared to the beautiful woman, not even trying to keep the envy out of his voice.

It had taken a lot of years, and even more well-traveled miles, for Mitchell Jade to confront his own demons and admit that he'd never had a home, a haven, a safe place where he could be exactly what he was.

"My grandmother has been eagerly awaiting your visit," Jessie admitted as he led the way toward the large bedroom at the back of the house. She stuck her head around the door frame and said quietly, "Grandmama, Mitch is here." To him she suggested, "Go on in. I'll be just a minute." Then she left, and he pushed the door open a bit wider and entered the bedroom.

Christine was as he remembered her. A little slip of a woman with silver hair and the bluest eyes he'd ever seen. What was it about the women of this family? They all had the most incredible eyes.

"Mitch."

Just the way she said his name made him feel wanted, appreciated, accepted, loved. Yes, loved. It was there in her voice, her eyes, the expression on her ageless face.

"Christine, I've missed visiting you." And he meant it. He hadn't realized how much until this moment.

"And I've missed you. You haven't been to see me for nearly two weeks."

Mitch sat down in the chair beside the bed and gathered her softly wrinkled hands in his. "It's been a busy two weeks at the university."

A simple unadorned understanding "Yes."

Then he remembered. "I stopped at Popplewell's on the way over here today. I have a little something for you." He reached into the pocket of his leather blazer and took out a small white sack.

Christine's eyes brightened. "Peppermint sticks?"

Mitch nodded. "Along with Mr. Popplewell's 'say howdy to Christine for me.'"

"Dear, dear Horatio Popplewell—" there was genuine affection in her tone "—such a fine young man."

Mitch laughed lightly under his breath. *Fine young man?* The storekeeper was seventy if he was a day. Aloud, he said to her, "Horatio? As in Horatio Alger?"

"Yes, the very same. Of course, the Popplewells had a family tradition of christening their eldest son Horatio long before the name became famous because of the writer. Or so I hear. That was before my time, naturally."

"Naturally."

She deftly changed the subject. "I haven't had a peppermint stick in ages."

Mitch could take a hint. "Would you like one now?"

"It's almost teatime."

He glanced at his watch. "Almost."

She furrowed her brow. "It might ruin our appetites—then Jessie would certainly scold."

"Right now I could eat a horse, maybe even two," he said drolly. Adding, "And don't worry, if there's any trouble I'll take care of your granddaughter."

"In that case, let's break a stick in half," she suggested. "You can have one piece and I the other."

Opening the paper bag, Mitch removed one stick of the red-and-white striped candy. He snapped it into two equal pieces and handed one of them to the elderly woman propped up in the antique bed.

"You did that very neatly," Christine said as she accepted her share.

"It's all in the wrist," Mitch replied with a grin.

Their smiles slowly faded; the room grew quiet for a moment.

Something flickered behind the aging blue eyes, now slightly myopic. "So you've finally met Jessie."

"Yes, I've finally met Jessie."

"What do you think of her?"

"She's lovely." He could tell that wasn't going to be nearly enough for Christine. "I've only spoken briefly with your granddaughter on one other occasion besides this afternoon, but she seems like an intelligent woman."

"She is that."

He went on. "She's feminine and attractive and obviously very successful."

Noncommittally, "Very successful—in some ways."

Mitch stared down at the peppermint stick in his hand. He suddenly felt ridiculous. A man didn't come right out and say: *I want your granddaughter more than I remember wanting any woman, even though I've spent ten, maybe fifteen minutes tops in her company.*

There was a strange fullness in his throat that prevented him from swallowing, yet his voice was controlled and only a little ragged around the edges when he spoke. "I like her, Christine."

"I knew you would."

"I like her a lot."

"I suspected as much."

"But it doesn't make any damned sense." He glanced up and muttered apologetically, "Sorry about that."

She ignored the profanity. "Why are you upset?"

He raised his eyes heavenward. "Because I met Jessie exactly twenty-four hours ago, for crying out loud."

"It can happen like that."

His eyes were two hard pieces of jade-green stone. "Not to me."

The old woman was gentleness itself. "*Even* to you."

He took a deep breath and decided to be truthful with her. "I'm no good for a woman like Jessie."

An incredibly sweet smile transformed the wizened face. "I wonder why men, in what they deem to be their infinite wisdom, are always making that claim?"

"What claim?"

Christine gave his hand a maternal pat. "Never you mind. Just remember that my granddaughter is an adult. You let Jessie be the judge of whether or not you're any good for her."

He shook his head from side to side and couldn't prevent a sarcastic, "Right."

Her touch was comforting. "Give it time, Mitch. You've both got plenty of time now."

"Yeah, plenty of time."

"Promise me just one thing."

His chin came up; his gaze was direct. "Anything."

"Give Jessie and yourself a chance." The fragile form in the bed shuddered with a sudden chill. "Promise?"

He nodded, his face darkening with concern. He held the small hand gingerly in his. "I promise, Christine."

The bedroom door opened behind him and he heard Jessie say in a lightly teasing tone, "I hope your promise to Grandmama has something to do with *not* eating those peppermint candy sticks before teatime."

Chapter Four

My Indiana Home

"I'm the one who promised to find my grandmother's high school yearbook. You don't have to come with me, you know," Jessie informed the man beside her as she opened the door to the third-floor attic.

"I know. But you also said that no one has been up here in years. Who knows what evil lurks—" Mitch gave the word a sinister twist "—amidst the dust and the cobwebs."

Jessie laughed. "I deal in antiques, remember? Dust and cobwebs are part of my business."

He bestowed a charming smile on her. "So they are. Then I'll just come along to keep you company."

"You're going to get dirty," she warned, having had the sense herself to change into a pair of slacks and an old sweater after they'd finished their tea.

Mitch glanced down at his faded jeans and white dress shirt and said to her, "I've been around the world a couple of times, and I've certainly been dirty before. Believe me, a little dust isn't going to matter."

"Suit yourself."

Single file, they climbed the flight of narrow stairs to the third floor of the farmhouse. They stopped at the top of the steps and looked around.

Late afternoon sunlight was flooding into the room through a row of windows on one end of the house. It gave a warm glow, a golden patina, to the large dusty attic and its contents.

Jessie heard herself say aloud, "There is something rather wonderful and peaceful about this place. I used to love to come up here when I was a child. I would play with the discarded toys and look through the stacks of old photographs and newspapers."

Mitch gave a noncommittal grunt and ran his fingers over the keys of an ancient Smith-Corona typewriter.

She went on. "One day I came across a trunk filled with Grandmama's letters and keepsakes. There was a book inside, too, carefully wrapped in layers of white tissue paper. It was well-worn and obviously well-loved. I took it out and crawled up into a rocking chair. I seem to recall that there were several spindles missing from the back..."

Expectant eyes turned to her. "And—?"

"And I began to read. I read the whole book before I fell asleep in that rocking chair." She pointed toward the far corner of the attic.

Mitch paused in his perusal of an old-fashioned black candlestick telephone that was sitting on a rather rickety table beneath the row of west-facing windows. "Must have been one heck of a good book."

Jessie nodded her head. "It was. I've never forgotten the thrill of reading *A Girl of the Limberlost* for the first time."

"A girl of the what—?"

"Limberlost. That was the name of the swamp in the story. The novel was written by an author from Geneva, Indiana—Gene Stratton Porter. She had a number of bestsellers at the beginning of this century."

"How old were you at the time?"

She raised one eyebrow in a sardonic arch. "At the beginning of this century?"

"At the time you read Porter's story," he clarified.

"Nine."

"Nine years old." The tone of his voice caught her attention. "I can almost imagine what you must have been like."

"Can you?"

"Yup," Mitch replied, settling in a straight-back chair and casually stretching his long legs out in front of him.

Suddenly he seemed too big for the room, Jessie noted.

He elaborated. "At nine you would have been tall for your age, on the slender side, I think, with a braid of chestnut-brown hair that reached halfway down your back."

"French braids, actually."

He ignored the interruption and continued. "Surprisingly grown-up, as only children tend to be."

"A lucky guess," she interjected.

"Intelligent. Undoubtedly a straight-A student in school. On the quiet side. A lover of books even then—" he tapped his chin thoughtfully "—with a secret dream of becoming a dancer."

"You've been talking to my grandmother."

"No, I haven't. At least not about your childhood. Why? Am I right?"

She hated to admit it, but—"Bingo."

A huge grin spread across Mitchell Jade's face. It seemed to Jessie that he was inordinately pleased with himself.

He tried to explain his success. "It's a certain knack we journalists acquire after years of working in the field," he said, not altogether serious. "I was, after all, once awarded a Pulitzer Prize for investigative reporting."

So it *was* true. She looked at him challengingly. "That might explain a lot, but how did you know about my secret dream of being a dancer?"

He leaned back in the chair and folded his arms across his chest. "It's your body. The way you move. Elegant. Graceful. Like a ballerina."

She was taken aback. "I—I see."

"And there's something about the way you hold your head." He tried to demonstrate with his own, and failed. "Maybe it's your neck."

Jessie felt the color rising in her face. "What's wrong with my neck?"

"Nothing. Absolutely nothing."

Jessie could tell he meant what he said. It was there in his eyes. Admiration. And a whole lot more.

Momentarily flustered, she began to rattle. "Did I mention that it turned out *A Girl of the Limberlost* was my grandmother's favorite book when she was a girl?"

The front legs of the chair hit the attic floor with a resounding thud. Like a man with a purpose in mind, Mitch slowly unfolded his arms and got to his feet. He walked straight toward her. "No, you didn't mention it."

"Well, it seems it was one of the few novels her strict Quaker parents approved of."

He came closer.

"They were very keen on natural history, you see." Jessie tried not to lose her train of thought. "Natural history was—ah—acceptable because it wasn't—frivolous.''

Mitch stopped directly in front of her. He reached out and, with apparent casualness, encircled her throat with his hand. "There is absolutely nothing wrong with your neck," he repeated in a voice suddenly gone husky with desire. "In fact, it is the most perfect neck I believe I've ever seen."

She swallowed and considered thanking him for the compliment. It seemed a little ridiculous under the circumstances since Mitch was going to kiss her, she realized in the split second before he lowered his head.

His lips were a fraction of an inch from hers when he paused. She could feel the warmth of his breath on her cheek. She knew he could detect her pulse beating wildly beneath his fingertips. Her palms were pressed against his chest, not pushing him away or urging him closer.

He murmured against her mouth, "Jessie, I want you to kiss me."

She shivered, and obeyed.

He hadn't said "I want to kiss you" like most men would have. She found that curious, and later, thought about it for a good long while.

She would wonder, too, why she had been so quick to do as Mitch asked. Perhaps it was because she'd wanted to kiss him as much as he'd wanted to be kissed.

But in that moment between not kissing him and kissing him, she was only aware of her own curiosity, of her own anticipation, and of his. Her last rational thought was that no kiss had ever lived up to her expectations.

She kissed him, and suddenly she forgot how to think, how to act, how to breathe.

She kissed him, and suddenly she was afraid. Afraid of both herself and him.

She kissed him, and suddenly he was kissing her back, his mouth smooth and strong on hers, her throat aching. His fingers made a gentle collar around her neck. His thumb found the small hollow at its base and lightly stroked back and forth as if to ease the ache. She thought she heard her name and his whispered between them, but the pounding of her heart drowned out all other sounds.

Her arms found their way around his neck; her hands unwittingly discovered the sensitive spot where spinal cord met nape. She threaded her fingers through the hair there until Mitch shivered hard and quick within her embrace.

The kiss more than lived up to her expectations. In truth, she couldn't even recall what her expectations had been anymore.

As the first kiss naturally led to a second and a third, it dawned on Jessie that there was a genuine sensual pleasure in touching this man. Pleasure and excitement and danger. The danger of forgetting who she was and where they were, what they were supposed to be doing.

"Mitch..." Could that low raspy voice possibly be hers?

Reluctantly he raised his head. "Yes, Jessie."

She put some small distance between them. "This isn't the reason we came up here."

"It might not have been yours..." He left the rest unsaid, but they both understood all the same.

She gave a nervous laugh and slipped out of his embrace. "I think I can imagine what kind of little boy you were like at the age of nine."

He stood with his feet planted a good eighteen inches apart, hands on hips, John Wayne style. "Do you?"

"Yes. Incorrigible."

Patiently he waited for her to continue.

Jessie ran her hand along the painted surface of a child's rocking horse. She gave the toy a push and watched as it teetered back and forth on the uneven floorboards. It seemed that Mitch was taking her claim seriously.

She said the first thing that came to her. "You would have been tall for your age, with a mop of dark brown hair that had yet to turn black, the same arresting green eyes, only at nine still wide-eyed, still innocent."

Mitch's blue-black brows, the same color as his hair, drew together. "I was never an innocent, even at nine."

Jessie looked up at him. "No. I suppose you never were." Then she turned and strolled across the room, stopping in front of a ladies' mirrored vanity. She studied her reflection, then his in the mottled looking glass. "Surprisingly grown-up, as the eldest child in a large family tends to be."

"A lucky guess," he said, parroting her earlier response to his comment.

"Intelligent, but undoubtedly *not* a straight-A student in school."

He showed his teeth in a sardonic smile. "Bingo."

She wasn't finished. "On the quiet side, but a fighter even then—" she searched his eyes "—as some children have to be in order to survive."

"You've got to know how to fight if you live on the streets," was all Mitch would say.

Her voice lost its sparkle, even to her own ears. "I think you were a loner, Mitchell Jade, with dreams of getting out and getting away. Which you apparently did at sixteen." More than anything Jessie hoped she was wrong; somehow she knew she was right.

Green eyes narrowed. "Yeah, well, there are dreams and then there are dreams."

She wasn't sure what made her ask. "Have your dreams come true?"

He hesitated. "Some of them have. Some not. Like everybody else's." A moment passed. "What about you?"

She looked at him blankly.

He tried a slightly different tack. "What about your dreams?"

Jessie walked to a sun-streaked attic window and gazed out across the far green valley, the one her family affectionately called the Happy Valley. She took in a deep breath, then let it out again. "For a long time now I've been searching for something, Mitch. I'm not sure I can put a name to it. Maybe it's peace of mind, maybe it's serenity, or simply a feeling of belonging somewhere. Anyway, I think I've found it at last, back in my hometown." She turned for an instant and flashed him a half-apologetic smile. "This is going to sound terribly sophomoric and sentimental, but it's a mistake to think that you can't go home again. I should have come home a long time ago."

"Home," Mitch repeated without a trace of inflection in his tone.

Jessie raised the index finger of her right hand and traced a random pattern on the dusty window pane. "Yes, home. This is where I belong. And this is where I intend to stay." She wiped her hand on her slacks. "What about you? Do you ever go back to that small town north of Philadelphia?"

"I did once. Ten years ago. For my mother's funeral."

There was a countable silence.

"I'm sorry, Mitch."

"No reason to be," he said in a voice devoid of emotion. "We weren't very close."

"What about your father and your brother and sisters?"

He answered with a kind of cold finality. "It's better for all of us if I keep my distance."

She sighed, unconsciously straightening her shoulders. "I'm sorry."

"For what?"

"For bringing up the subject of your family when it's obvious you'd rather not talk about them."

There was an intractable expression on his face. "I don't have much to say about my family, that's all."

That wasn't all, but Jessie recognized it was time to back off.

She tried to instill a sufficient amount of enthusiasm for the task ahead into her manner. "Well, I guess I'd better start looking for Grandmama's high school yearbook."

Mitch nodded in agreement. "Do you have any idea where it is?"

She stopped and looked around. "It's in one of these trunks. I think."

"You think?"

She gnawed on her bottom lip. "Logic dictates that it must be."

He appeared skeptical. "Does it?"

"You're the Pulitzer prize-winning investigative reporter. What do you think?"

Mitch was silent for a moment, evidently mulling it over. "I think logic dictates that your grandmother's yearbook is in one of these trunks."

Jessie laughed. "Which one?"

"Eenie. Meenie. Minee. Moe." He pointed at a large brown trunk of indeterminate age and origin. "That one."

"I suppose it's as good a place as any to start," she mumbled under her breath.

Going down on her haunches, Jessie brushed a few cobwebs aside, undid the thick leather straps and pushed the lid of the trunk open. It was filled with photograph albums, bundles of old letters stuffed into shoe boxes, newspaper clippings and faded yearbooks. There was a slightly musty scent to the whole lot.

Mitch hunkered down beside her. "As I was saying earlier, it's a certain knack we journalists acquire after years of working in the field."

She gave him a telling glance and began to sort through the stack of yearbooks, reading the embossed dates off the front of each. "1931. 1954. 1946. 1922. 1917." She stopped and more closely examined the last one, repeating, "1917." Opening to the flyleaf, Jessie found, written in a carefully schooled hand, her grandmother's maiden name, Christine Brick. "This is it," she announced triumphantly.

"That didn't take long." He seemed almost disappointed.

She wrapped her arms around the yearbook. "We got lucky."

"Lucky? Luck had nothing to do with it," Mitch declared with a certain amount of male arrogance.

She wasn't about to argue with him. "Whatever you say, Mr. Jade."

"Here, I'll close that for you."

While he did up the leather straps on the large brown trunk, Jessie spotted for the first time a slightly smaller and markedly older one behind it, shoved back into a dark dank corner of the attic. The Saratoga-style trunk was covered with dust. It looked as if it hadn't been opened in years, possibly in decades.

Jessie set her grandmother's yearbook aside and dragged the antique trunk out under the natural daylight of the windows. She looked around and found a piece of cloth and dusted off the top. Then she slowly opened the lid.

Weeks later Jessie would wonder what path her life would have taken if she had simply retrieved the yearbook, walked back down the attic steps and left well enough alone that afternoon.

But she didn't.

In the end, that one seemingly insignificant act made all the difference.

As she opened the long-forgotten trunk, her scalp began to tingle. The tiny, infinitesimal hairs on the back of her neck were standing straight on end. All of her senses seemed heightened.

She could detect even the smallest sound inside and outside the third floor of the farmhouse: the barely perceptible scratch of a tree limb against a window pane, the wind playing in the topmost branches of the great Golden Raintree atop the hill, the scuttle of a mouse in a far corner of the room, the regular, rhythmic breathing of the man beside her.

She inhaled deeply. The air in the attic was warm and dusty and slightly stale, yet there was a familiar underlying odor of mothballs to it all.

And something else...

She took in another deep breath. It was Mitch, of course, and the distinctive combination of scents she had quickly come to associate with him: a subtle, woodsy after-shave, a faint hint of leather, the spice and honey of the tea cake from earlier that afternoon, and something—something a little wild, something indefinable.

Jessie drew her attention back to the trunk. The surface felt cool beneath her fingertips as she slowly raised the lid. The pungent odor of camphor and mothballs hit her square in the face. There was a piece of muslin serving as a cover. She carefully pushed it to one side to see what was beneath.

"Good Lord."

"What is it?" inquired Mitch from behind her.

The breath was caught in her lungs for a moment. Her voice was hushed. "Baby clothes."

She gingerly removed the first garment as if it were as precious to her as it must have been to the woman who'd placed it in the chest for safekeeping. The small gown was Quaker plain, but each stitch was perfectly and lovingly sewn by hand.

"I wonder whose they were," said Mitch, voicing her own sentiments.

"I don't know. There are just a few things here—a gown, a bib, a tiny crocheted sweater, several crib blankets. It's as though they were put aside as a keepsake, a mother's memorial." Jessie tightened her throat against sudden inexplicable tears. "Judging from the style and the material I would guess that they're at least one hundred years old."

Beside her, Mitch sat back on his heels. "That old?"

"Yes."

"I wonder what else is in the trunk," he said, reading her mind.

Jessie carefully placed the baby clothes on the piece of muslin before exploring further.

"A batch of old letters," she speculated as she handed a stack of yellowed envelopes to Mitch.

He opened the first one and informed her, "The date is April 2, 1849. It's written to 'Mama' and signed 'Thy loving daughter, Mary.'"

"1849. Thy loving daughter, Mary," Jessie repeated thoughtfully. "I believe that's the same Mary who stitched the quilt on Grandmama's bed."

"Which would make the Mary of these letters your—"

"—great-great-grandmother," she finished for him as she uncovered a large box at the bottom of the trunk.

"Let me help you with that," Mitch quickly volunteered.

Jessie waited while he removed the box and placed it on the table beneath the windows. She steadied herself and then removed the top.

"It's a needleworked sampler," she said, once the first of the box's contents was revealed.

He peered over her shoulder and read aloud the name sewn into the homespun material. "Elizabeth. 1812."

Reverently Jessie ran her fingertips over the delicate piece of stitchery. A feeling of happiness and contentment seemed to steal over her. "I believe Elizabeth was a very happy child back in 1812 when she stitched her alphabet and numbers."

There was an undertow of fascination in Mitch's voice. "This is the same Elizabeth who originally settled the homestead with her husband, isn't it?"

Jessie wet her lips with her tongue. "Yes."

"A genuine Carolina lady, the wife of a gentleman farmer, that's what Christine told me once." He seemed to remember something. "She met Johnny Appleseed. Did you know that?"

Jessie smiled. "No, I didn't." Taking a beautifully bound leather volume from the same box in which they'd discovered the sampler, she said, "This appears to be Elizabeth's diary."

As she opened the journal, there was no feeling of intrusion, no sense of wrongness or of playing the voyeur. There wasn't even a hint of what this step into the past would mean to her own future.

The book simply fell open to a page and Jessie began to read in Elizabeth's elegant hand:

July 10, 1821

The wolves do howl so at night. 'Tis a lonely and haunting sound. I often lie awake and think of all the dear souls we have left behind. I do feel like a Stranger in a Strange Land. Will this Indiana wilderness ever seem like home?

July 25, 1821

An Ohio man is going around the County preaching to anyone with half a mind to listen. 'Tis said when he isn't preaching he's planting trees and herbs, or brewing teas and poultices. His name is John Chapman and he seems a cheerful sort of man and Godly. I gave him a bowl of rabbit stew.

August 17, 1821

I have been thinking. Once the land is cleared per-

haps I will ask Joshua to plant me a small apple
orchard.

August 29, 1821

Tonight after supper I stood at our cabin door and
looked across the green, green valley. I could see
the blue mist on this summer's eve as it drifted toward me. For the first time since Joshua and I left
Carolina my heart has ceased its yearning. This is
our home now. This is my Indiana home.

"My Indiana home," echoed Jessie.

She looked up from the journal and gazed out the
attic window at the green, green valley in the distance,
the same green valley that Elizabeth Banks had gazed
out at from her cabin door one hundred and seventy
years before.

She tried to keep the quiver out of her voice. "Sometimes the past isn't very far away. That's what my
grandmother told me only yesterday. She's right, isn't
she?"

Mitch's voice sank to a caressing whisper. "Yes. She
usually is, I've found."

Jessie could feel him standing behind her, watching
her, waiting for her. Solid. Substantial. Unknown, yet
familiar. Dangerous, but desirable. Violent, but capable of great gentleness, as well.

She glanced back at the diary in her hands. It had
flipped ahead a few pages and she caught a glimpse of
something on a background of white.

A name.

She quickly looked up, not trusting her own eyes, in-
sisting to herself that she'd only imagined it.

Her shoulders stiffened.

Apparently Mitch noticed. "What's the matter?"

She managed to tell him, "I'm not sure."

Bracing herself, she looked down and quickly read what was written in the journal. Then she turned to Mitch. She knew her eyes were huge with apprehension.

He gripped her arms. "What is it?"

"Nathaniel."

"Nathaniel?" Recognition took a second or two. "What about Nathaniel?"

Jessie's voice was shaking slightly. "I think I know who he is."

Chapter Five

Home Sweet Home

"I think I know who he *was*."

"*Was?*"

"Yes. Listen to this." Then she read aloud to him again from Elizabeth Banks's diary:

September 14, 1821

A stranger has come to the County. He has admitted to my husband that he served with General Jackson against the British back in '15. Since we are of the Friendly Persuasion and do not abide fighting & war & killing our Fellow Man, he thought it necessary to tell us he had been a soldier. Joshua says it was the honourable thing to do. Perhaps that is so. All the same, I do not think the stranger is a Gentleman.

September 26, 1821

Joshua has taken to calling the new man by his Christian name. I was asked to do likewise. But I refused, telling him, "Thee knows I cannot. It would be most unseemly."

We have taken the newcomer on since we cannot clear the heavily forested land by ourselves. He
is a hard worker, to be sure. But there is something about Major Nathaniel Currant that dis-
turbs me greatly.

Her voice trailed off. She tried to swallow and found
her throat was dry. "What do you think?"

Mitch scowled, his mouth turning down at the corners. "I don't know, Jessie."

She pleaded with him. "Please tell me what you
think."

He seemed to put off giving her a straight answer for
as long as he could. "I think you're jumping to some
pretty wild conclusions."

"Wild conclusions—"

"You've got to admit there are a dozen explanations
that make more sense."

Her lips folded into a softly obstinate line. "Maybe."

He seemed to be choosing his words carefully. "It's
more than probable that you met somebody called Nathaniel when you were a child, and his name has been
buried all these years in your subconscious."

"I don't think so."

"Then you could have read the name somewhere, or
heard it on the radio, or TV or even at the movies."

"But—"

He held up a hand to stop her. "The fact that Elizabeth wrote in her diary about an ex-soldier named Nathaniel doesn't explain why you called me Nathaniel in
Popplewell's store yesterday afternoon."

Jessie stared at him, her voice sinking to a bewildered whisper. "Is that what I was doing? Calling *you*
Nathaniel?"

Mitch ran his fingers through his hair in an agitated gesture as he paced back and forth across the attic floor. "I'm pretty sure that was the case. I went over it again and again in my mind last night, and I'm convinced you thought I was Nathaniel. Whoever he is." He blew out his breath expressively. "Frankly, there isn't one shred of evidence linking your Nathaniel to Elizabeth Banks's Nathaniel."

Jessie was stung by his skepticism. "But there is."

"There is?"

She stared at him mistrustfully. "I didn't tell you everything yesterday," she admitted. "I was afraid you'd think I was crazy."

Mitch's manner was one of masculine indulgence. "I know you're not crazy, honey."

Her pulse was wildly erratic. She blurted out, "I actually saw Nathaniel for a moment."

That stopped Mitch dead in his tracks. His head shot up. "*Saw* him?"

Her breath came fast. "I saw a man dressed in buckskin, carrying a rifle in his hand. There was a backpack strapped to his shoulders. He was wearing a wide-brimmed hat on his head. His hair was long and dark brown—it curled at the back of his neck. There was something in his eyes—" Jessie closed hers and tried to recall exactly what it had been "—but I can't seem to remember..." She opened her eyes. "I guess that's all."

Mitch muttered a short explicit oath under his breath. "I take back what I said about knowing you're not crazy."

Jessie froze. Then she raised herself up to her full height and informed him, with genuine desperation in her voice: "I am not a fanciful woman, Mitchell Jade. This kind of thing has never happened to me before. I don't have an explanation for it, but I am most certainly not crazy."

Immediately he was apologetic. "Hey, I didn't mean anything by it. Honest."

She said with a touch of reproach, "I'm sorry I told you."

"Look, it was a stupid crack to make, all right?" A slightly self-mocking smile edged his mouth. "God knows, I've seen plenty of strange things in my life that seem to defy logic. I've always prided myself on keeping an open mind, of going into any given situation without preconceived ideas. It's essential for a journalist." It was obvious he could have kicked himself. "I'm sorry, Jessie."

With the toe of her loafer, she nudged a dustball in a haphazard fashion across the floorboards of the attic and finally relented. "Apology accepted."

"Why don't you tell me everything you remember, exactly as it happened?" he suggested.

Rather unwillingly, she did just that.

Afterward, Mitch cleared his throat and confessed, "I don't know what to make of it."

"You're not the only one," said Jessie ruefully. She had to admit the story sounded ridiculous. "Since I don't believe in ghosts or anything remotely of the kind, I can only conclude that Nathaniel must have been a figment of my imagination."

His arm was gentle across her shoulders. "I'd have to agree with you."

She found a scrap of paper and marked the spot in Elizabeth's journal. "Still, 'there are more things in heaven and earth, than are dreamt of....'"

He gave an noncommittal shrug. "*Julius Caesar?*"

"*Hamlet*." Then she managed in a light casual tone, "I guess we'd better be getting downstairs."

"Are you going to take these other things with you?"

She nodded. "The box of Elizabeth's keepsakes, as well as Grandmama's yearbook. The sampler should be framed under glass to preserve it and protect it properly. And I'd like to read more of the diary."

Mitch had been quiet, in a thoughtful kind of way. He said now, "So would I."

She raised one brow. "Would you?"

"Yes."

She was curious. "Why?"

He hesitated, then shrugged. "Elizabeth has fascinated me from the first time your grandmother told me about her."

Her brows came together in a small line. "Elizabeth, Joshua and Nathaniel," she recited their names in a whisper.

"The eternal triangle?"

"I don't know." Jessie gave him an uncertain glance, just as a shiver of excitement raced through her. "But I intend to find out."

"I REMEMBER NOW," Christine announced as she and Jessie were sitting on the front porch enjoying an unusually warm afternoon for the first week of May.

Taking a sip of iced tea from the tall frosted glass in her hand, she asked, "What do you remember, Grandmama?"

The answer was given with complete aplomb. "Who Nathaniel was."

Behind rose-tinted designer glasses, Jessie's eyes grew round as saucers. She gave the older woman her full attention. There was an element of expectancy in her voice. "Who was he?"

"A soldier."

"In what war?" she asked, sitting very erect beside her grandmother's wheelchair.

For a minute the question was pondered. "It would have been the War of 1812. He joined up with the Tennessee militia and served under Andrew Jackson. When General Jackson was sent to defend New Orleans, Nathaniel went with him." The silver-capped head moved from side to side as Christine recalled with dismay, "It was said they fought bravely and well that January of 1815 against the British. It wasn't until the battle was over and won that they found out a peace treaty had been signed two weeks before."

Jessie hesitated, weighing her words. "How do you know so much about Nathaniel?"

Christine gazed out at the farmyard and beyond to a cluster of small red barns, giving it about thirty seconds of thought before answering. "I read about him in Elizabeth's journal."

She had to remind herself to stay calm. "You've read Elizabeth's journal?"

"Oh, yes."

"You've never mentioned it to me."

"Haven't I?"

"No."

"It must have slipped my mind. It was a long time ago."

Jessie was brimming with questions. "About Elizabeth's diary—"

A subtle change came over the frail woman in the wheelchair. "Perhaps it is best if you discover the contents for yourself." No further explanation was forthcoming. "Now will you answer a question for me, my dear?"

"I'll try."

Christine cut straight to the heart of the matter. "Why the sudden interest in Nathaniel?"

Jessie wondered how much she should say. The last thing she wanted was to upset the person dearest to her in the world. Especially when that person was nearly ninety-two years old and in fragile health. At the same time her grandmother had always been able to tell when she was lying.

She decided a compromise was in order.

"When I was up in the attic with Mitch looking for your high school yearbook, I discovered Elizabeth's journal at the bottom of the Saratoga trunk. As I removed it from the storage box, the pages fell open to an interesting passage about Johnny Appleseed. That's when I happened to notice the name Nathaniel."

It was all true; it just wasn't all of the truth.

Christine listened politely, then insisted, "But that was *after* you'd already asked me about Nathaniel. Don't you remember, my dear?"

Jessie shook her head guiltily.

"You came home from Popplewell's one afternoon. It was the same afternoon you first ran into Mitch. And you asked if I knew anyone named Nathaniel. I recall thinking at the time that I should know who he was. But I couldn't seem to place the name. That was the day *before* you went up into the attic."

Jessie tried to finesse the situation and failed. "Was it?" she said weakly.

There was absolutely nothing wrong with her grandmother's memory at times.

"Yes, it was." In a kind gentle voice, she was asked, "Do you want to tell me about it?"

"I'm not sure I should," Jessie said, with a touch of anxiety.

"I'd understand."

She began to fidget in her chair. "I don't think so."

Her grandmother tried to smooth over the moment. "I promise to listen and not judge."

Unshed tears suddenly burned in her eyes. Jessie reached out and interlaced the blue-veined fingers with her own. For a few minutes, perhaps even longer, they simply sat on the front porch of the farmhouse and held hands: the old woman nearing the end of her life and the younger woman with so much of life still ahead of her.

"There isn't much to tell." A huge sigh. "It sounds crazy, anyway. Even Mitch thought so."

"You've told him?"

She threw her loose dark hair back from her shoulders. "That day in the attic."

"You're not certain you should have."

"You can say that again." She spat the words.

Christine said affably, "Mitch is usually such a nice man—"

"He tried to be nice about it, Grandmama. But, let's face it, Mitchell Jade and I are strangers. He doesn't really know anything about me."

With unshakable confidence Christine stated, "But I do, and there is nothing you can say that will make me love you any less."

She gave her grandmother's hand an appreciative squeeze. Her voice grew full. "I know."

"Go on."

She took in a sustaining breath and began. She told it all just as it happened.

When she was finished her grandmother said only, "Hmm."

Jessie drew in a long breath and let it out slowly. "I— I thought you'd be upset by what I've told you."

"I'm not in the least upset."

"I can see that." Her heart pounding in her ears, Jessie was driven to ask: "Why not?"

Her grandmother turned slowly, staring into her eyes. "Because I once had a similar experience in Popplewell's myself."

She was dumbfounded. "You, Grandmama?"

"Me. Perhaps I should explain."

Jessie experienced a brittle sort of calm. "Perhaps you should."

The words came from Christine Warren almost unconsciously. "It was the autumn of 1917. I was in Popplewell's doing some shopping for Mama when I saw the shadowy figure of a young man. He appeared to be dressed in the uniform of a World War I doughboy. Then the uniform changed, and I recognized the symbol of a red cross on the man's arm."

Jessie leaned forward eagerly.

"My vision was blurred, but even so I realized I knew the young man. It was my older brother, Charlie, and he was wounded. I could see the bloodied bandage wrapped around his chest. He was obviously in great pain."

"Dear God."

The episode was related matter-of-factly. "I tried to speak to Charlie. It seemed very important that I make him understand—Lord only knew about what." Her grandmother hesitated. There was a measure of silence. "James found me there a few minutes later on the floor of the general store. Apparently I had fainted."

"And—" Jessie prompted, sensing there was more to the story.

Christine sighed. "James had been sent to fetch me home. It seems a telegram had just arrived from France where Charlie was a volunteer ambulance driver. Our family was being notified that he was a patient in a French hospital, and was in critical condition. While serving near the front lines, he had sustained a severe bullet wound."

Jessie's dark liquid eyes were filled with empathy. "To the chest?"

"To the chest."

"Just as you saw in your vision."

"Just as I saw in my vision."

It was some time before Jessie ventured in a shaky voice, "Is it ESP? Some kind of sixth sense? Some psychic ability we have?"

"I don't know."

"It has to be more than mere coincidence."

"I agree."

"Perhaps there is a special bond between the women of our family," murmured Jessie. "Some kind of predisposition passed on from one generation to the next."

"Perhaps."

"There is a socio-biological theory that claims memories are passed along in genes like eye color. A particularly sensitive person might be aware of these memories."

Christine looked confused.

"It would be as though you had amnesia and then slowly began to recover your memory."

"I don't know, Jessie. In all my years it has happened to me no more than a few times, not even a handful. It only seems to come during moments of great emotional trauma, and not always then." In a beautiful voice, her grandmother added, "Perhaps my sister, Hannah, described it best. She told me it was a gift, a gift that comes from having an understanding of the human heart."

Jessie's mouth twisted. "A gift or a curse?"

"It's natural you should feel that way. I know I did in the beginning. Later I grew to believe it was whatever you make of it."

Jessie lowered her head. "Whatever you make of it."

"All I can say is that you're not alone, my dearest. Through the years there have been many sensitive intelligent Friends who have written down their dreams and visions and premonitions—some joyful, some tragic. You are not alone, Jessie."

She didn't have the heart to tell her grandmother that she'd been alone most of her life.

After a time she said, "You were barely eighteen, Grandmama. How did you manage?"

The wise old woman said, "I managed because I had to. As women have always had to. As you will."

And somehow Jessie knew she would.

Later she remarked, "I wonder why it was Nathaniel that I saw."

"I don't know," admitted her grandmother.

"I suppose it'll become clear to me in time."

"I suppose it will."

"I believe the answer may be in Elizabeth's journal."

A firm directive was given. "Then that is where you should begin your search."

She ran her eyes over the figure in the wheelchair. "Are you getting tired? You know what the doctor said. Don't overdo it just because you're feeling a bit better."

Christine seemed unconcerned. "I'm fine. It's such a beautiful afternoon that I'm quite enjoying sitting here on the porch." She added, "You're expecting Mitch in a few minutes, aren't you?"

"Yes, I am." Jessie drank the last of her iced tea and rose to her feet. "I think I'll change into something a little cooler. Can I get you anything before I go upstairs?"

"No, thank you. You run along and change your clothes." Then, "Jessie—"

She paused with her hand on the doorknob. "What is it, Grandmama?"

"You do like Mitch, don't you?" came the gentle nudging.

"Like Mitch?"

Like was probably the last word she would have used in relation to Mitchell Jade.

She was curious about him, intrigued by him, occasionally mesmerized by his wit, his intelligence, his smile, his sensuality. She was even a little afraid of the man. There was a dark side to him that he took great pains to conceal.

Like Mitchell Jade?

No, she didn't like him. What she felt for him was much stronger than that.

But she could hardly say to her grandmother: *I find the man irresistible. His desire for me is a potent and seductive force.*

Instead, as she went into the house Jessie casually tossed over her shoulder, "Like Mitch, Grandmama? Yes, I like Mitch very much."

Chapter Six

Home Before Dark

He'd always wanted to kiss a pretty girl in a convertible.

The thought filtered through Mitch's mind as he downshifted into first gear and let the red sports car roll to a complete stop at the intersection of the two country roads.

He nonchalantly stretched his arm out along the back of the leather seat and turned to Jessie. "I like your hair that way."

"Thank you."

"Most women would insist on wearing a scarf or something to keep it from blowing all over," he observed.

Jessie made an expressive face. "I can't stand having anything confining on my head. Hats, scarves, even barrettes bother me."

He reached out and wound a strand around his index finger. It was even softer and silkier than it appeared. "You have such lovely hair," he murmured, his voice dropping half an octave. "It'd be a shame to cover it up."

His passenger seemed intent on changing the subject. "Are you sure you don't mind running all over the countryside with me?" she asked.

Mitch returned both hands to the steering wheel. "Nope, I don't mind. It's a perfect day to put the top down and cruise. Besides, the salesman at the Corvette dealership said I should break in my car gradually." He shifted gears again and took off along the blacktopped road. "Your wish is my command. Just tell me where to go," he shouted over the roar of the powerful engine.

"Don't tempt me," Jessie shot back playfully.

"I meant as in 'give directions.'"

She made a production out of biting the inside of her mouth, and muttered with a touch of dry wit: "So did I."

Mitch put his head back and laughed, savoring the sensation. "Where to first?"

"I'd like to stop at Seth Hillock's. He and his wife, Alice, have an antique shop on Old Spiceland Road. They used to be the best in the business when it came to appraisals and restoration. I assume they still are. I want the Hillocks to be the ones to frame Elizabeth's sampler."

He watched out of the corner of his eye as Jessie took a pair of dark glasses from her handbag and slipped them on.

"Turn left at the next intersection and follow the road south for a mile or two," she directed.

"Yes, ma'am."

Five minutes later she announced, "There it is." Jessie pointed out a large white barn with the words HIL-LOCK'S ANTIQUES stenciled in black on the side.

"I swear every other barn, shed or garage we've driven by has been converted into some kind of antique shop," he said, turning into the driveway.

"Antiques are big business around here," Jessie informed him.

"I might expect that to be true of New York, or London, or even Paris, but small-town Indiana?"

The woman sitting beside him seemed to be in comfortable, familiar territory now. "During the great migration west the pioneers often got this far and realized that they couldn't haul Great-aunt Gertrude's chest of drawers all the way to California or Oregon. So they'd sell what they couldn't manage to carry, or sometimes just dump it by the side of the road. That's one way the midwest became a gold mine of antiques."

"What are the others?"

Jessie went on. "Like thousands of Quakers my ancestors came to Indiana at the beginning of the last century. There were some wonderful carpenters and cabinetmakers among them." She leaned closer and said, "Do you recall the table in the front hall at Grandmama's?"

He thought for a moment. "Yes. Very plain and simple. Utilitarian, but beautifully made. Reminds me a little of the Shaker style."

"It was made in 1886 by my great-grandfather as a wedding gift for his bride. In those days furniture was built to last, and it has. Now we call them antiques. Of course, there are a few lucky people like Grandmama and me who still have in their possession the family heirlooms and keepsakes first brought to this country. There's a tea service in the dining room that one of our great-greats hauled from England, as well as a few pieces of family silver."

Mitch watched the animated expression on her face. Jessie was so alive, so vital, when she talked about her passion for antiques. "You're fascinated by the past, aren't you?"

She gave a decisive nod of her head. "I always have been. One of my favorite lines is by William Faulkner. It goes something like, 'The past isn't forgotten. It isn't even past.' That's how I feel."

"You must have learned an incredible amount about history along the way."

"Perhaps not the kind you find in the history books, but, yes, I have. Of course, like most antique dealers I've had to specialize. My area of expertise is nineteenth-century English porcelain and silver."

He was curious about her business. "What about your antique shop in New York?"

"It's not mine anymore. I sold out to my partner last month."

Mitch watched her for any outward signs of regret. "You're really not going back."

She didn't hesitate for a second. "I'm really not going back. I'm in Indiana for good."

He pursued the same general line of questioning. "What will you do here?"

"To start with, just look after my grandmother and enjoy the first real vacation I've had in years." She grew thoughtful. "Later on, I may open a small shop, or simply rent a booth in one of the antique malls."

"Antique mall?" The words evoked a strange mental image.

"I'll show you after we visit the Hillocks. It happens to be the second stop on my list."

Mitch pulled into an available parking space alongside the converted barn. He opened the door of the sports car, carefully unraveled his long legs and climbed out.

He heard his passenger clear her throat. "Kind of a tight fit, isn't it?"

He quickly glanced down at the faded blue jeans clinging to his thighs, and explained, "I guess they must have shrunk in the wash."

This time it was Jessie's turn to laugh. It began in the back of her throat and bubbled up through her lips—a delightful sound, unguarded and thoroughly contagious. It brought a smile to his face.

"No—" That was apparently all she could manage before another spasm of laughter shook her shoulders. "I meant the Corvette."

"Oh—the Corvette." Then, feeling a little foolish but not really minding, Mitch began to laugh, too.

THEY WERE STILL LAUGHING as they sauntered into the Hillocks' antique shop.

"Jessie!"

"Alice, how wonderful to see you."

"Seth, look who's here. It's Jessamyn Jordan," his wife announced.

A big grizzly bear of a man came toward them. He had a full beard and thick shaggy eyebrows, and his hair was as much white as it was brown. "My word, girl, it's good to see you."

Jessie turned and included the man standing on her right in their conversation. "I'd like you both to meet Mitchell Jade. He's teaching a course over at the college. Mitch, this is Alice and Seth Hillock. They gave me my first job in the antiques business when I was sixteen."

The gray-haired woman said, "We always considered Jessie our star pupil, too. She was one of those people who just seemed to have a knack for antiques."

"Speaking of which, this isn't purely a social call," she told her old friends and employers. "I have something in Mitch's car that I'd like the two of you to look at if you have a few minutes."

Alice answered for both of them. "We'd be glad to."

They were all gathered in Seth's office before Jessie carefully opened the box with the sampler inside.

"My, my," murmured the diminutive woman as she peered over her spectacles at the piece of antique needlework.

"You can say that again," muttered Seth as he reached for his magnifying glass.

Alice Hillock turned on a high-intensity lamp at her elbow while her husband centered the box on a huge desk that partially served as a worktable. She opened a drawer and took out a pair of pristine white gloves. She slipped them on before touching the sampler.

"Homespun," he said succinctly. "Thread's authentic. Look at that shade of red."

"Natural dye," his wife concluded.

"The border design of birds and flowers is traditional for the time period," Seth went on. "Well-executed but by no means expert."

Alice offered her opinion on the subject. "Stitched by a child, or possibly a young girl."

He read aloud the lettering at the bottom of the sampler: "'Elizabeth Finished This Work In The Eleventh Year Of Her Age 1812.'" Then he mumbled to himself for a minute or two, seemingly oblivious to his guests. "Look at the 's' in the word 'finished,' Alice."

"I believe I've seen lettering like that recently in a reference book on antique English samplers," she told him.

They both glanced up at Jessie.

"My ancestors were originally from England," she confirmed.

"This Elizabeth was your—"

"—great-great-great-grandmother."

"The sampler is wonderful," enthused Alice Hillock. "I've only seen a handful older than this one. They're usually in museums these days. You're very fortunate to still have yours in the family."

Jessie was gratified. "I know."

Seth gave her a slightly disapproving look. "The only thing I'm wondering is why it hasn't been preserved properly."

"As a matter of fact, Mitch and I just discovered the sampler in an old trunk in my grandmother's attic."

Seth just shook his head from side to side and scratched his beard. "Don't rightly know if I could put a value on your great-great-great-grandma's needlework," he advised. "Appraisers and auction-house experts are always at odds with each other, as you know. The value of a sampler like yours depends on so many things—fabric, color, dye, technique, style, age, how rare the design is." The man shrugged his massive shoulders. "The first thing you ought to do is get it framed under glass, or at the very least wrapped in clean cotton and stored in an acid-free box."

"That's why I brought Elizabeth's sampler to you and Alice. I'd like to have it framed, and you always were the best in the business."

The former farmer furrowed his bushy eyebrows. "It'd be a genuine challenge, Jessie. Although the material looks in pretty good shape." A muscle in his face started to twitch. "Could take me some time. The shop's been mighty busy this spring and the tourist season is just about upon us."

Her reply was reasonable. "I can wait for as long as it takes."

Seth turned and began to search the crowded shelves behind him. "Believe I have a partial wood frame from the early 1850s I could repair and use for the job."

A youth stuck his head around the door of the office and said, "Excuse me, Mr. Hillock, but there's a couple from Pennsylvania out here with a question about the price of those stoneware jugs and crocks."

"Be right there, Virgil," he called back.

"You see to your customers first," urged Jessie.

"I'll get to the framing as soon as I can. You mind leaving the sampler with us now?"

It's what she'd intended to do. "No."

"You put it safely in the house, Alice, where it won't be bothered none."

"Yes, Seth."

He was halfway out the door when he paused and said to his stock boy, "Introduce yourself to these folks, Virgil. I'll see to the customers."

Virgil was tall, red-haired and painfully thin. He had slender, slightly stooped shoulders and a bad case of teenage acne. He approached Jessie and tentatively held out his hand. "I'm Virgil Marquart. I work for the Hillocks."

"Jessie Jordan. And this is Mitchell Jade." She smiled and tried to put the gangly youth at ease. "Have you worked for Alice and Seth long?"

He blushed for no apparent reason and shook his head. "Just started in April. I, ah replaced Becky Sue

Stoots when she had to quit because she couldn't lift stuff or be on her feet all day on account of she's pregnant."

"My grandmother has known Becky Sue since she was a little girl," volunteered Jessie. "I didn't realize she and Lyman were expecting a baby."

Virgil Marquart nodded his head and stuck his hands in his pockets. "They are. Come September. Not that they couldn't use the extra money from this job. Lyman doesn't have any medical insurance and things are real tight for local farmers this year." He blushed again. "At least that's what I heard Becky Sue tell the Hillocks when she came by to pick up her last paycheck."

Jessie turned to Mitch and said, shaking her head, "The girl can't be more than seventeen or eighteen, herself."

"You must be talking about Becky Sue," deduced Alice Hillock on her return to the office. "It's a sad story. I don't mean to sound unsympathetic, but the girl had no business getting pregnant in the first place. Times are hard. Lots of folks are unemployed. At least she had a steady job here with us."

Jessie opened her mouth to respond and closed it again without comment. She'd only been back in town for a few weeks. She wasn't going to get herself embroiled in local gossip.

"We'll let you both get back to work," she told Virgil and her former employer. "We've got some other stops to make this afternoon. You let me know if Seth runs into any problems with the sampler."

"Sure thing, Jessie. Don't be a stranger now."

"I won't be," she assured the woman as they left.

They were nearly to the outskirts of town before Jessie leaned toward Mitch and asked him, "What did you think of the Hillocks?"

His eyes were squinted against the afternoon sun. "They're nice enough. Not very sympathetic when it came to Becky Sue Stoots, though, whoever she is."

Jessie thought about it for a minute. "Alice and Seth are the salt of the earth—hardworking, practical, not in the least sentimental. They never had any children of their own. And they certainly don't suffer fools gladly. I suppose they think Becky Sue and her husband are a bit foolish, that's all."

"For having a baby?"

"For not waiting to have a baby. They're young and they're dirt poor. You heard Virgil Marquart. Apparently they can't even afford the medical bills."

Mitch's back grew rigid. "Two strikes against the kid and he hasn't even been born yet."

Jessie looked at him out of the corner of her eye. The scowl on his face told her that his sympathies were definitely with the unborn child.

What was it Esther Huckelby had said the day Mitch came to tea?

The housekeeper's words came back to haunt her: *You can always tell the ones who've had to fight for every scrap they got. There's something about them. Something in the eyes.*

Well, Mitchell Jade's eyes were a deep, dark, resentful green. Somehow she didn't think his own childhood had been a very happy one.

Of course, the decision to have a baby wasn't always based on logic, Jessie reflected. It could have been an accident in the case of Lyman and Becky Sue. Either way, there had to be something she could do to help the young couple. She'd have a chat with her grandmother about the Stoots. Yes, that's what she would do.

"What's this antique mall you're taking me to?" inquired Mitch, breaking into her thoughts.

"It was once a huge, sprawling Victorian house, dating from the mid-1870s, and added onto and renovated countless times in the decades since," she said. "Initially built by a prominent family in town, it became a boardinghouse during the Depression, and was finally turned into an antique mall about twenty years ago."

"An impressive building," exclaimed Mitch as he parked in front of a huge structure with FENNER'S lettered above the front entrance.

"A house this large must have been considered a mansion in its day," said Jessie. "The current owner is Thesslong Fenner. Or at least it was. Grandmama told me only today that Thess died last winter and his nephew from New Jersey inherited everything." Her tone was disapproving.

Mitch couldn't resist teasing her. "So, an outsider has moved in and taken over."

She gave him a telling glance. "We simply like to know with whom we're doing business."

"*We?*"

"We locals." Her nose went up in the air a fraction of an inch. "I was born in New Castle, after all."

"I guess that makes you a native daughter."

She tried to explain. "A lot of things are settled with a handshake in a rural community like ours. A man's word should be as good as his bond. No one in New Castle really knows much about this David Fenner, that's all."

Mitch chuckled under his breath and came to David Fenner's defense. "He's probably a harmless young

man with a pretty wife, a thirty-year mortgage and a
prematurely receding hairline.''

ONE LOOK.

That's all it took for Mitch to form an intense dislike
for David Fenner.

The man was too smooth, too handsome, too young
and *far* too interested in Jessie from the moment they
walked in the front door of the antique mall.

Still, Mitch consoled himself later, he had remembered to mind his manners and shake the other man's
hand while the introductions were being made. Once the
niceties were out of the way, they did their level best to
ignore each other.

The young Fenner gave Jessie a smile that literally
oozed with charm and showed all of his perfectly cap-
ped snow-white teeth. ''I heard you were back in town.
I've been looking forward to meeting you. I can see that
everything they say about you is true—and more.''

Mitch watched as a hint of color crept up Jessie's
neck and onto her cheeks. Good grief. She wasn't some
gullible teenager; she was a full-grown woman. Surely
she recognized that David Fenner was what they com-
monly called a ''smooth operator,'' and about as genuine as his teeth.

Jessie extended her hand. ''I was sorry to hear about
your uncle. I worked here at the antique mall one summer during high school. Thess was very—kind to me.''

Mitch heard the slight catch in her voice and wondered what had happened that particular summer. He
decided to make a point of asking her about it later.

She added, ''I was fond of Thess. We all were. He'll
be missed by the people of New Castle.''

The handsome blond Adonis held her hand in his, far longer than was required, and drawled in an intimate tone: "Yes, we'll all miss dear old Uncle Thess. He was quite an endearing character, wasn't he?"

Mitch just bet old Thess was. His nephew wasn't doing too badly in that category, either.

"Do you mind if we look around?" Jessie asked the antique mall's new owner.

"Not in the least. In fact, I have a few minutes before my next appointment. It would be my pleasure to give you a personally guided tour."

"That really isn't necessary," she told him.

"I insist," said the man, with yet another charming smile, as he buttoned the jacket of his designer suit and closed the door of his office behind him.

A personally guided tour *was* completely unnecessary, Mitch grumbled to himself. Anyone could see that Jessie knew her way around the rickety old house as though it was the back of her hand. She frequently greeted the other dealers by name as the three of them strolled from crowded room to crowded room, poring over pieces of antique furniture, fragile china teacups, moldering quilts and rusting doodads. Mitch didn't think he'd ever seen so much "stuff" in his entire life.

"So your specialty is English silver and porcelain," David Fenner was saying to her as the two of them discussed their mutual interest in the business of antiques and collectibles. "Then you're not an expert on Americana?"

"Not in the least," Jessie admitted. "Naturally, I've picked up some information from my grandmother over the years. We have a number of nice pieces out at the farm. Not that she thinks of them as antiques. They're family keepsakes to her, and to me."

Their host paused by a flight of grand stairs that wound up to the second story of the huge Victorian house, and gazed down at Jessie with a particularly ingratiating expression on his handsome face. "Naturally."

He offered her his arm and they walked up the steps, their heads bent in conversation: Jessie's darker chestnut brown one beside David Fenner's salon-styled golden blond.

It was some time later that Mitch heard Jessie inquire, "Do you have any booths available for rent?"

"We have a waiting list at the moment...." He caught the calculated look in Fenner's baby-blue eyes. "Why? Don't tell me *you're* interested in renting a booth?"

She laughed lightly. "I might be."

It was smoothly suggested, "In that case, I think something can be arranged."

Mitch didn't want *anything* arranged. He didn't want Jessie to be anywhere near David Fenner if he could help it. He didn't like the guy. Not one bit.

The two of them walked on ahead. Mitch stopped on the second-story landing and stood there, staring into space.

It wasn't like him to take such an immediate and intense dislike to someone. What was wrong with him, anyway?

Then the answer to his question hit him square in the face, like a blast of icy cold air. Cripes! He was jealous. In fact, he was jealous as hell.

"Well, I'll be—!" Mitch muttered under his breath as he shook his head from side to side.

So, the green-eyed monster had finally reared its ugly head and bit him but good. Jealousy was a funny thing, it turned out. Funny as in curious, not humorous. It didn't say much for him as a journalist that he'd allowed his emotions to so easily cloud his judgment.

But jealousy was a new and unique experience for him. He didn't think he'd felt this way in his entire thirty-six years. Well, maybe once back in the tenth grade. He couldn't even remember the girl's name now.

There might have been one other time, but he couldn't seem to recall any of the details....

He had learned to trust his instincts about people in the long years since high school. There was something about David Fenner, something he couldn't quite put his finger on. It didn't have anything to do with Jessie, or being jealous of the other man.

At least he didn't think so.

"Would you be free to join me for dinner this evening?" The invitation was being issued as he caught up with them.

"Thank you, but—"

"—but I'm afraid we can't," Mitch finished on Jessie's behalf. He casually slipped an arm around her shoulders and looked from one to the other. "We already have plans for tonight. Right, sweetheart?"

"Y-yes, I suppose we do," she agreed, darting an odd look at him.

There was a flash of perfect white teeth. "Perhaps another time, then."

"Perhaps," answered Mitch. Then he glanced down at the watch on his wrist. "Gosh, Jessie honey, look at the time, will you? We'd better be on our way."

"What was that all about?" Jessie demanded to know as he hurried her out of the antique mall and into the low-slung sports car.

He growled out of sorts, "Nothing."

"Mitch, the truth."

He firmly shut the door on the passenger side and circled the red Corvette. "The truth is I don't like the guy."

"But you've only just met him."

He'd refuse to talk to her about it if she was going to insist on being logical.

She drove her point home, quoting him verbatim. "You were the one who said David Fenner was probably a harmless young man with a pretty wife, a thirty-year mortgage and a prematurely receding hairline."

Mitch was fully prepared to eat his words. "I was wrong." On all counts, as it turned out.

"David seemed nice enough to me. It was kind of him to give us a personally guided tour of the mall."

Mitch didn't think kindness had anything to do with it.

He got behind the wheel and inserted the key in the ignition. "I don't like David Fenner. I don't think his word is his bond, or whatever it was you said before we went inside."

"As good as his bond."

"Yeah, that's it, as good as his bond." He wasn't about to admit that David Fenner's smooth, Ivy-League good looks made him feel like a bungling clod.

Mitch glanced down at his hands and realized he was gripping the steering wheel so tightly that his knuckles had turned white. He loosened his grip and took a deep breath.

He wasn't sure later what made him say it. He told himself that he wasn't testing Jessie, that it didn't have anything to do with the fact David Fenner was standing at his office window watching them.

In the end, he didn't care what his reasons were. He only knew one thing. He wanted to kiss Jessie. And a whole lot more. But he'd settle for a kiss right now.

He arched a brow in her direction and said baitingly, "You Quakers are very big on telling the truth, aren't you?"

"Yes, we are."

He slid his fingers around the back of her neck and felt an immediate response as she shivered with awareness. He liked what he could do to Jessie with just one touch. "Honesty is always the best policy?"

"Absolutely."

Mitch deftly dropped his bomb. "In that case, would you like to kiss me again?"

Her eyes widened appreciably. "You mean now?"

He leaned toward her. "Yes, I mean now."

"Here?"

"Right here." He watched the full play of emotions on her face: surprise, confusion, interest and desire. "The truth," he reminded her.

Jessie toyed with her sunglasses. "All right." She swallowed with obvious difficulty. "Yes, I would."

Relief poured into his veins. Like good Scotch whiskey, it was heady stuff. "Good, because I've always wanted to kiss a pretty girl in a convertible."

Her eyes were a deep, rich, sherry brown as they gazed up into his. "With half the town watching?"

In a stormy undertone, he said, "I don't care if the *whole* town is watching." He moved closer.

She didn't flinch. "But I do. I have to live here long after you're gone, Mitch."

He stopped. "Dammit, Jessie, I want you." He started the car, put it in reverse and backed out of the parking space.

"Where are we going?" she asked as he sped down the street.

He slowed to the legal speed limit. "To my place."

She brushed the hair away from her face. "I promised my grandmother I wouldn't be late."

"Don't worry—" Mitch turned and stared into her eyes "—I'll have you home before dark."

Chapter Seven

A House Is Not a Home

"I don't have to be home before dark. I'm not a child."
Jessie was annoyed with him and took no pains to conceal it. "I only meant that I don't like being out late because my grandmother sleeps lightly and she'll be disturbed if I come in after her bedtime."

Mitch mumbled something that sounded vaguely like "sorry" and kept his eyes straight ahead.

Jessie slipped her sunglasses back into place and did likewise.

What was wrong with Mitch, anyway?

First there had been that funny business with David Fenner, who, despite her initial misgivings, had turned out to be a charming man. Then there was the matter of their abrupt departure from the antique mall, followed by the scene in his car when Mitch had asked if she wanted to kiss him.

Jessie's brows drew together in a thoughtful frown. She gnawed on her bottom lip. Mitchell Jade wasn't an easy man to understand. Of course, what man was? The entire male sex was unfathomable at times.

Then it suddenly occurred to her. Why hadn't she thought of it before? This magnificent man sitting beside her was *jealous*; jealous of a pretty boy like David Fenner. She was momentarily stunned.

As he pulled up to a stop sign on a shady residential street, Jessie was tempted to lean toward him and whisper reassuringly in his ear: "I've changed my mind. I want to kiss you, Mitchell Jade, even if the whole town *is* watching."

She inched closer.

There was a stubble of black hair on his chin and on the hard angular jut of his jaw: five o'clock shadow. For the first time she noticed that his ears were perfectly shaped and neatly fitted to his head. His hair was long in the back and brushed against the collar of his shirt, but it wasn't unattractive.

She inched a little closer.

His eyes were squinted against the late-afternoon sun; there were crow's-feet at their corners. She could see a hint of color, then a glorious sunburst of yellow and lighter iridescent green around the darker jade of his irises.

She was about to open her mouth and speak when Mitch shifted gears and they took off down the street. She'd hesitated and the moment was lost.

His house was on the other side of town, just off State Road 3, due north of Memorial Park and the Raintree Heights subdivision. It was huge and modern, a magnificent structure made of stone and plate-glass windows that overlooked a small meandering stream and a patch of dense deciduous trees. The wood was already thick with new growth; it would be nearly impenetrable by the end of the summer.

Mitch unlocked the front door and Jessie walked ahead of him into the house.

It was empty.

That was Jessie's first overwhelming impression. There was not one stick of furniture in sight: not one rug on the plain hardwood floor, not one painting hanging on the expanse of white walls, not one plant basking in the sunlight that poured in the windows. Not even a pair of drapes or a set of window blinds was in evidence from where the two of them stood in the cavernous entranceway.

She was puzzled. "Have you just moved in?"

"No," answered Mitch, rubbing his chin thoughtfully. "I've been here for about six months now."

Six months! Her jaw dropped in amazement.

Mitch seemed to realize, perhaps for the first time, that his house was different from most houses, certainly from hers. He explained, "I didn't see any reason to fill the place up with furniture and knickknacks if I'm not staying. Besides, I like wide open spaces."

This was more than simply wide open spaces, Jessie wanted to say. This was cold and impersonal and lonely. This was a house, not a home. She took two deep shuddering breaths and resisted the urge to wrap her arms around herself.

"You're not staying in New Castle, then?" she said, picking up on something he'd mentioned in passing.

He eased his key chain into the front pocket of his jeans. "I'm not sure yet."

"I suppose a small town seems...small—if you're used to bright lights and big cities."

"Yeah, I suppose it does," said Mitch neutrally.

"And the academic life requires a certain kind of personality, a certain amount of steadfastness and maturity."

"It's different," was all he would allow. He added: "The university has made an attractive offer. I've got a few more weeks to make up my mind."

"I see," she said with simplicity.

There was an uncomfortable moment.

"C'mon, I'll give you the nickel tour," volunteered Mitch, taking her by the elbow and guiding her toward the rear of the house. "This is the great room, according to the rental agent, anyway."

"It's magnificent," exclaimed Jessie as she gazed at the massive room with its twenty-foot-high cathedral ceiling.

The walls were painted the same stark white as those in the entranceway. A solitary chair and an oversize sofa were plunked down in front of the fireplace; they were also white. Otherwise the great room was empty.

"The furniture was here when I moved in," Mitch tossed over his shoulder, as if that somehow explained everything.

Jessie noticed there were only occasional intrusions into the colorless decorating scheme: the subtle browns and muted oranges of the native limestone used to construct the fireplace and hearth, the bare wood floors polished to a dark sheen, the matching brass light fixtures on the wall.

All of the color was outside: emerald moss growing on the black bark of a tree, a glint of yellow sun, a slice of pure blue sky and the endless variegation of green, everywhere green.

"This is one of the largest rooms I've ever been in," she observed. "And I know that's the largest fireplace I've ever seen." The chimney soared two stories and more into the air, covering the entire wall at that end of the great room. "I'll bet it's wonderful with a fire going."

He was silent. Then: "I don't know. I haven't used the fireplace yet."

She didn't say "that's a shame," although it was. She did stand in front of the mammoth fireplace and study the mantle above it, running her hand along the bare stone.

"I'm surprised you don't display a few of the souvenirs you must have accumulated during your extensive travels."

The expression Mitch turned to her bore no trace of apology. "No souvenirs. I travel light. I prefer it that way."

Jessie thought about it.

No furniture.

No knickknacks.

No souvenirs.

No wife, past or present, according to Grandmama. No children. No family. No real home. It seemed that Mitchell Jade did travel light. Very light, indeed.

If she were smart, Jessie reminded herself, she wouldn't get involved with this man. In the end, he'd leave and her heart would surely be broken.

Why couldn't she listen to the sage advice, then? Instead she poked her head around the corner of the next room. "What's in here?" she inquired.

"I guess you'd call it my study."

The study, at least, looked occupied. Most of the available space was taken up by a leather-cushioned office chair and a large desk. The desktop was covered with books and papers. There was a reading lamp in one corner. Several cardboard moving boxes were scattered around the floor. Some were open, some not. They seemed to contain more books and papers. There was a computer, as well. The screen was blank, but there was a stack of hand-scribbled notes next to it.

"Writing your memoirs?" she teased.

Mitch's features altered. "As a matter of fact, I am." He threaded his fingers through his hair in an absent-minded gesture. "At least I'm trying to, anyway. They aren't really my memoirs, more like a collection of observations I've made during my years as a reporter."

"I'll bet you have dozens of fascinating stories to tell," she said sincerely. "A reporter would surely view the world from an entirely different perspective than the average tourist."

"You can say that again," he muttered.

She paused by the desk, one hand brushing against a pile of thick hardcover books. In a bemused voice she read the titles out loud: "*The Myth of Democracy in Modern China, Eyewitness to History, A Country Made By War: From the Revolution to Vietnam—The Story of America's Rise to Power, Crossroads of Modern Warfare.*" She wetted her lips with her tongue and said in a lightly ironic tone, "Not exactly bedtime reading."

Mitch's eyes began to shimmer. "Perhaps not. But incredible, previously even unthinkable, changes have taken place in the world in the past few years, Jessie."

She faced him, smiling but quite serious. "And you were there."

"And I was there." There was an unmistakable ring of truth to his words as he continued. "I literally saw history in the making. I witnessed events that people should know about—the assassination of Benigno Aquino at the Manila airport back in the summer of

'83, the massacre of the students at Tiananmen Square, Romania, the war in the Gulf.''

She spoke her thoughts aloud: "You were there and saw all of that . . . that horror and violence?"

He reached out and for a moment cupped her chin in his palm. He looked into her eyes before he confirmed, "Yes, I was there and saw the horror and the violence. The blood. The killing. I have seen the atrocities carried out in the name of Allah, of Buddha, of God." There was both disdain and disillusionment in his voice.

Mitch walked back into the great room. He stood and stared out the windows in the rear of the house. His profile was etched in dark relief by the sunlight. The thumb of one hand was looped through his belt, the other hung at his side.

Jessie followed him. She wanted to reach out and touch him, comfort him, but she was afraid to.

His voice grew louder, echoing through the empty room. "I don't believe that Allah, or Buddha, or God, had anything to do with it, or ever has. It's a legacy, a legacy of hatred and violence, of pain and prejudice, that we so-called human beings have passed on from one generation to the next, for tens, for hundreds, for thousands of years. Sometimes I think we should do ourselves and our children a favor and blow ourselves off the face of the planet."

"Surely there is always hope for the human race, Mitch."

His shoulders slumped. "I used to think there was."

"Used to?"

He opened his arms wide and let them fall in the classic gesture of defeat. "I had such high ideals when I started out, Jessie. I finished my GED while I was in the navy and worked my way through college after I was discharged. I chose journalism because I thought it was a way to make a difference. I was going to report the facts, the truth with a capital T. I was going to make the world see itself as it really was, and help it to change. Now..."

"Now what?"

There was a kind of cold finality to his voice as he slowly turned to her and said, "Now I know that the facts and the truth aren't even the same. That the world doesn't want to see itself as it is, that it has no intentions of ever changing."

There was a great throbbing heartbeat caught in her throat. "That's a very cynical attitude."

He folded his arms across his chest and gazed down at her. The skin around his mouth was taut. "I thought you knew, sweetheart. I'm a very cynical man."

She suddenly felt like crying. "Oh, Mitch—"

He was adamant. "It's true, Jessie."

"Is that why you quit working as a reporter and came to teach at the university?" she asked with a certain grim understanding.

He shrugged his shoulders. "I thought I might be able to make a difference with a classroom of college students."

"I think you can make a difference, even if it's just with one person."

He frowned. "One person?"

She tried to explain. "Sometimes in the end it all comes down to one man and one woman, Mitch. They make a difference with each other, and the world is changed, just a little, for the better."

His face darkened. "Not always. Not every man and woman who are foolish enough to fall in love are any good for each other, or for the people around them.

Look at the divorce rate in this country. Or worse, the statistics on spouse and child abuse. Good Lord, half the women who are murdered in the United States are killed by their husbands or boyfriends. So much for love 'until death us do part.'"

Jessie tried to appear calm, but tears were pricking the back of her eyes. She wasn't reaching him. She wasn't sure she ever could, or would. "I know there are a large number of dysfunctional families, but there are a lot of warm and loving ones, as well."

"Dysfunctional families—now there's an interesting catchphrase." Mitch's dark brows came together in a single black line. "What would a nice Quaker girl like you know about dysfunctional families? You grew up in a home filled with love and peace, in an atmosphere of tranquillity and harmony. That has been your heritage as a Friend." He sighed. "I only hope you appreciate it."

"Of course I do."

"Some of us weren't so lucky. Our family heritage was one of alcoholism, domestic violence and abuse, or at the best, neglect."

Her pulse was suddenly wildly erratic. "Was your family like that?"

Mitch looked at her for a long hard while before he answered. "Yes."

There was the taste of something acerbic, something bitter that lingered in Jessie's mouth. She tried to swallow and couldn't; her mouth was dry as a bone. She tried to find the right words to say to Mitch, and there were none. It was what she'd feared all along: he had been an abused child.

She suppressed a shudder. "How awful for you."

"Yeah, it was awful."

"Is that why you never see your family?" she asked so softly that she could barely hear herself.

He sounded almost savage as he spat out a succinct "Yes."

Then it occurred to her. "Is it the reason you've never married?"

"One of the reasons," admitted Mitch, his mouth turning slightly self-mocking. "I've always been afraid to get married, assuming any woman would be nuts enough to have me."

"Afraid? Why?"

"Because I believe we recreate our parents' relationship in our own, our childhood in our childrens'. Pick up any article or book on the subject of family dynamics and you'll find that the professionals agree with me." His green eyes narrowed. "I have no intentions of passing on to my own children the hate, the violence, the abuse I knew as a child."

She laid her hand on his arm and said, "You wouldn't, Mitch. You're too fine a man. Too intelligent. Too sensitive. Too loving. I don't believe you would ever harm your own wife and children."

"Nobody can guarantee that," came the brutal reply.

"There are no guarantees for any of us," she declared in an impassioned tone. "But it isn't unheard of for a determined adult to create a family life that is the *opposite* of what he knew as a child."

"Maybe." He eased his arm out of her grasp. "But you said it yourself, Jessie—the past is never very far away."

He was twisting her words, or rather, Grandmama's words.

"Human beings can change, Mitch, if not their past, then surely their future. I believe that with all my heart."

He persisted. "I'm still not willing to risk it."

She heard him, incredulous. "You really are afraid." She was understanding, perhaps for the first time, just how powerful the past could be.

"I've already said I was."

Jessie did not back down. She stood her ground. "We're all afraid of something."

He challenged her. "What are you afraid of?"

"I'm afraid that everything I love will end up dying," she said after a moment, struggling to keep her voice even.

"Your parents died one summer while you were in high school, didn't they? The summer you went to work for Thesslong Fenner at the antique mall?"

"Yes. How did you know?"

Eyes of vivid green rested thoughtfully on her. "It was something you said earlier this afternoon."

Jessie was willing to tell him about it. "I was seventeen when they volunteered as Quaker missionaries to Ethiopia. My father was going to teach conservation and farming techniques. My mother, health and English."

"Were they always teachers?"

She nodded. Then she stood beside him and stared out the windows at the green woods, unaware of the faraway look in her eyes, or the wistfulness in her voice. "They signed up for a three-year stint. Sometimes I was terribly lonely without my parents, but they believed in what they were doing. They said it was important."

He stiffened with disapproval. "It was important for them to stay home and raise their own daughter, too."

She reminded him, "I was nearly grown by then. In another year I would be going off to college, anyway." There was a long moment of silence. "It was the summer of 1978 when we were notified that my mother and father had been killed during the fierce fighting that took place between government troops and secessionist guerrillas in the Ethiopian province of Eritrea."

She heard his intake of air.

"It was impossible to have their bodies returned home, of course. They were buried in Africa. So far away, so very far away," she said in a small dismayed voice. "It hit my grandparents hard. My mother was their youngest child."

"It must have been hard for you, too."

She forced herself to speak. "Yes, it hit me hard, too." She took a fortifying breath, determined to finish her story. "I told my grandparents that I wasn't going away to college, after all. I would live at home with them and commute to classes. There's an exceptionally fine Quaker school only thirty-five miles from New Castle."

"Earlham College. Yes, I'm familiar with its reputation," he said.

"They insisted I follow my original plans and so I went off to Swarthmore the following year. Eighteen months later my grandfather died. Now all I have left is Grandmama."

Although unspoken, it was there between them: the knowledge that her grandmother was dying, as well.

Mitch's face momentarily darkened. "What a fine pair we make."

"We do make a fine pair," she said, knowing full well that he hadn't meant it. "We've both survived some bitter disappointments. We're successful. We do whatever we can to help other people. We believe in trying to make the world a better place in which to live."

He clasped her softly but firmly by the upper arms. "You are a beautiful, intelligent, desirable woman, Jessamyn Jordan. You're a creature of peace and love, goodness and generosity. It's not often that I try to be noble, so don't throw it back in my face."

She gulped. "All right."

He gave her a little shake and released her. "I'm warning you off in the nicest way I know how. Trust me, sweetheart, if you're smart you won't have anything to do with the likes of me. I'm no damned good for you."

Jessie had told herself the same thing only minutes before. But it wouldn't be the first time that she hadn't followed her own good advice.

She caught the tip of her tongue between her teeth. "I think I should be the judge of that, don't you?"

The man's mouth hardened. "Not if you're a lousy judge of character."

Jessie refused to give up. It wasn't in her nature. And Quakers could be just as stubborn as the next person, she wanted to inform him.

After a while she simply whispered, "Do you believe in God, Mitch?"

"I don't know. I guess so."

"Do you believe in Fate?"

He fell silent, musing. "You mean preordained events?"

"Yes."

"No, I don't."

"What do you believe in?"

Mitch held up his hands, examined the palms, then lowered his hands again. "I believe that life is a gamble, a series of random chances."

There was a glimmer of hope, after all, Jessie assured herself. "Does a belief in random chance detract from the basic miracle of two people finding each other among all the millions of inhabitants in our world?"

He lifted his broad shoulders.

"I don't think that it does."

She could see she had his attention.

"So?"

"Some people are *meant* for each other, Mitch, and they know it practically from birth. My grandparents, for example. My grandfather first saw Grandmama on the day she was born. Can you imagine that?"

His shoulders began to relax a little. "No. That's pretty amazing."

"We both know not everyone finds happiness with the boy or girl next door. The path to finding each other is more difficult for some, not so obvious. Yet those two people are meant for each other as surely as the sun rises in the morning and sets in the evening."

"Why, Jessamyn Jordan," he exclaimed, "I do believe you're a romantic."

She blushed. "I suppose I am."

"I should have known." He shook his head and chuckled under his breath. "I thought they were a dying breed."

"There are a few of us left," she said with dry amusement. Somehow the subject had gotten away from Mitch and was focused on her. Perhaps the past was simply too painful for him to deal with, even yet. If he needed to let it be, then she would let it be, as well.

At least for now. "Besides, what's wrong with being a romantic?"

"Nothing really," said Mitch as he moved toward her. "It's just that you don't see too many these days outside of poetry circles and college campuses, of course."

"Of course." She cleared her throat and took a step back. "How about the rest of my nickel tour?"

"This way." He directed her toward the second story of the house. "There are four—" he rubbed his chin "—or maybe it's five bedrooms upstairs. And several bathrooms. I only use the one at the end of the hall."

"The others are empty," she surmised.

She was correct. They walked past one empty bedroom after another until they came to the end of the hallway.

"This is the master suite, according to—"

"—the rental agent," she finished for him.

He gave her a lopsided grin. "Right."

The master suite was dominated by a huge platform bed that was three steps up and centered under a skylight in the roof. The bed was unmade; the sheets were rumpled and hanging half off the mattress. One over-size pillow had been tossed on the floor; the other looked as if it had been pummeled with a fist. There was a damp towel thrown across the foot of the bed and a pair of jockey shorts on the carpet.

"I—ah—wasn't expecting any visitors," Mitch said apologetically as he scooped up the discarded undershorts, threw them in the closet and closed the door.

Jessie managed not to crack a smile all the while.

Sunlight poured in through the skylight and a row of French doors that opened onto a balcony. The balcony faced the woods. There was a stack of books sitting on the floor by an overstuffed chair and an adjustable lamp beside it. That was all.

Still, there was something incredibly intimate about Mitch's bedroom, Jessie realized as they stood in the middle of the room. She was intensely aware of him, for one thing. As she had been that afternoon in the attic.

She turned and found him standing directly behind her. She said the first thing that popped into her mind. "You have a nice view from here."

"Yes."

Skittishly she asked, "Do you ever use the balcony?"

"Sometimes."

His monosyllabic replies weren't contributing much to their conversation. She gave him a quick sideways glance. He was staring at her. From this angle the scar on his chin seemed more pronounced. She wondered what had happened.

"Where did you get the scar on your chin?"

"I fell and cut it on the edge of a table. It was a long time ago."

There was obviously more to the incident, but she sensed this wasn't the time or the place to probe any deeper. She reached up and traced the jagged line with the tip of her finger. "Does it ever hurt?"

"No. Not now. It hasn't in years." His voice sank lower and lower with each word.

She reached higher and outlined the angle of his nose. "Did you really have your nose broken during a boxing match?"

"Yes. Twice."

"While you were in the navy?"

"That's right."

Mitch stood perfectly still and let her touch him and ask her questions. There was no expression on his face. Nothing in his eyes that she could detect. Just a slight softening of his mouth, and that was nearly imperceptible.

Drawn into a trap of her own making, Jessie murmured in a husky voice, "Have you really always wanted to kiss a pretty girl in a convertible?"

He reached out a lazy hand and followed the line of her bottom lip with his finger. "Yes, but who needs the convertible as long as you have the pretty girl?"

Then he bent his head and touched his tongue to the spot where his fingertip had been only moments before. It was a featherlight caress that tickled and tantalized at the same time. It lasted for only an infinitesimal second.

Her pulse doubled. "Are you playing games with me, Mitch?"

He placed both hands firmly on her waist and brought her up hard against him. "I don't play games, Jessie. It's not my style."

"It's not mine, either," she managed before her breath and reason deserted her.

"Good." Then he brought his face down to hers and, without further ado, covered her mouth with his.

He was delicious: the taste of him, the feel of him, the unique scent she knew was his and his alone. Jessie swore she would have known it anywhere.

She opened her mouth to murmur Mitch's name, and his tongue surged between her lips, plumbing the moist depths, engulfing her in a wave of sensuality that left her clinging to him. She wanted to crawl inside his body, to be a part of him from the inside out, to see through his eyes, to feel through his fingertips, to smell through his nose, to hear through his ears, to taste through his mouth. She wanted to *think* and *feel* what he was thinking and feeling. She wanted to understand how his mind worked, what made him the man he was, how he felt about her. She wanted to know a thousand things and more about him.

She made a frustrated little noise.

He drew back an inch, no more, and muttered, hoarsely, "What is it?"

"Nothing."

"Jessie, the truth."

She felt slightly demented. "I can't tell you."

"You can."

"I'm afraid to."

"There's no reason to be afraid."

Of course there was, she wanted to inform him. "I'm not very brave," she said instead.

"You are. You're very brave, and being brave means overcoming your fears," he murmured against her lips.

"Does it?"

"Yes. Tell me, what is it?"

She reached up and gently grasped his face between her palms. She gazed into his eyes. "I want to know what you're thinking," she finally declared. "What you're feeling. I don't want to merely guess. I want to *know* who you are."

Something seemed to snap inside Mitch. Maybe he'd been holding back, afraid he might frighten her away if she saw the true magnitude of his passion for her, the depth of his desire. Her words set something inexorable in motion. He picked her up and held her at eye level; her feet were dangling off the ground three or four inches.

"Mitch—" That quickly her breath had expired.

Then his mouth was on hers once again, his tongue entangled with her tongue, his hands on her waist, her hips, her breasts, and she forgot about breathing, forgot about everything but this man and the way he touched her. She knew only this moment, this place, this overwhelming passion. All else had no meaning, no reality for her. It began and ended with Mitch.

Heat radiated from him like a blazing log fire. She could feel the tension in his shoulders, the strength in his arms, the hardness of his body. He'd said he wanted her. There was no doubt about it under the circumstances.

He ground his hips against hers. Her breasts were flattened to his chest; his chest was like a brick wall. He covered her derriere with his hands and urged her closer until he seemed embedded in her flesh. Still, she wanted more and more, only more.

He instinctively located each and every one of her vulnerabilities, and she shivered with each and every caress. His hands were between them, moving across her abdomen in slow, sensuous circles. He found the small of her back, the spot just beneath her ear, the tips of her breasts.

She felt as though she couldn't breathe, as though the rug had been snatched from beneath her feet. She lost her balance and fell against him.

She put her head back and laughed drunkenly, wondering if she was making any sense. "Is this always part of the tour?"

"Oh, hell, Jessie." Mitch tore his lips away and rested his forehead against hers. She felt the quiver that ran down his body. "I'm sorry."

"I'm not. Not really."

He whispered at her shoulder. "We're not a couple of kids."

"No, we aren't."

"We should know better than to rush into— Into this."

She was feeling provocative. "Should we?"

He loosened his grip on her. "If there's going to be something, anything, between us, I want us both to go into it with our eyes wide open."

"Eyes wide open is always the best policy."

"Always. We've got to be truthful with each other, Jessie. It's the only way."

She put a palm against his chest, counting his heart-beats. "The only way."

"I want you," he said, his voice vibrating.

She took a deep shaky breath. "And I want you."

"I don't know how much longer I'll be staying in New Castle." A tense frown bracketed his lips. "I do know you're not the kind of woman a man casually makes love to and then leaves."

"No, I'm not."

He bit off his words sharply. "But I'm a man and I'm human. I think it'd be an excellent idea to leave this bedroom before I decide to say the hell with being no-ble and throw you down on the rumpled sheets and make wild passionate love to you."

She felt a hot blush wash across her cheeks.

Mitch's voice dropped to a caressing slur. "I've wanted to make love to you for such a very long time, Jessie. I know it doesn't make any sense, but that's how I feel."

"I feel the same way," she admitted.

Reluctantly he released her and retreated to safe neu-tral territory. It was several minutes before her breathing and his returned to normal. He suggested to her, "There's a little Italian restaurant just down the street. What do you say to a plate of lasagna and a glass of red wine?"

As they left his bedroom, she smiled halfheartedly over her shoulder at him. *"Si, signore."*

IT WAS NEARLY DARK before Mitch turned onto the country road that led to the Brick family farm. He pulled up in front of the house and killed the engine of the red convertible.

Jessie issued him a polite invitation. "Would you like to come in for a cup of coffee?"

"I don't think that would be a good idea."

Truth was, he didn't think he could take much more physical frustration tonight. He had to keep his hands off her. That's all there was to it. And if he went inside, one thing was bound to lead to another.

"I guess it is getting late."

He made his excuses. "Yes, it is. And I've got a whole stack of papers to grade before my first class tomorrow."

She put her head back against the leather seat. "In that case, thanks again for driving me all over the county this afternoon."

"Anytime."

"And thank you for showing me your house."

He gave a wry smile, but said nothing.

"Mitch—"

"Yes, Jessie."

She leaned toward him. A certain look came into her eyes. "I want you to kiss me."

He watched her in the fading light of day. "Here?"

"Here."

"Now?"

"Now." A brief smile flitted across her mouth. "I've always wanted to kiss a handsome man in a convertible."

"I don't know about the handsome part...."

Their lips met and it began all over again: the wanting, the desire, the need.

There was a hidden fire within this woman, Mitch reflected briefly as they kissed. He could feel her response through his mouth, his hands, his whole body. It was enough to drive a man mad....

He kissed her once and then she was gone, out of the car and up the porch steps. He thought he heard her say something just as she opened the front door and disappeared into the farmhouse. He must have been wrong. Jessie couldn't possibly have entreated: "Please don't break my heart again."

Again? He wondered if she'd asked him that before and he had ignored her plea.

It was still on Mitch's mind later that night as he stretched out on the huge unmade bed, one oversize pillow propped up at his back, hands folded behind his head. Outside the moon was full and, through the open French doors, his empty bedroom was awash with silver light.

Had he broken her heart before? And his own?

He was unable to sleep and unable to find any answers.

Chapter Eight

Far From Home

"'How far away, Philadelphia, P.A.,'" sang Jessie under her breath as she fastened the sheets to the clothesline strung up between two sturdy poles in the backyard.

Hanging bedsheets outside to dry was an old-fashioned custom that Esther Huckelby and her grandmother still subscribed to, along with taking cod-liver oil for your health and eating milk-toast if you were sick. She could—and did—decline to follow the precincts of the last two now that she was an adult, but the sheets were still hung out to dry whenever the weather permitted—which in Esther's book was any Monday it wasn't actually pouring rain or the temperature sub-zero.

The activity brought back a flood of happy memories for Jessie: a warm day in spring after months of winter cold, purple lilacs in bloom, their fragrance permeating the house, her room, her senses; the household traditions kept alive from generation to generation, the little touches her grandmother gave to her home just as the women in the generations before her had.

She paused in her singing and wondered if anyone had ever hung Mitch's sheets out to dry.

Somehow she didn't think so. The man had undoubtedly never known anything but machine-dried bedding, and that just wasn't the same. Nothing compared to fresh country air billowing through damp cotton percale.

Nothing.

A brief vision of Mitch's bedroom flashed through Jessie's mind: the huge platform bed centered under the skylight, the sheets rumpled and hanging half off the mattress, one pillow tossed to the floor, the other bearing the imprint of his fist, the intimacy of the time and the place, his kisses, her reaction to them.

She stepped into the shade cast by the side of the farmhouse to cool off for a moment. At the thought of Mitch her body began to grow warm again.

Mitch—with his slumberous green eyes and broad, muscular shoulders.

Mitch—with his deep, resonant laugh that sent little slivers of awareness sliding along her spine.

Mitch—with his soft, insistent mouth and urgent hands.

Mitch—when he wanted her, when he made her want him.

With the sleeve of her shirt, Jessie took a swipe at the perspiration on her face. Simultaneously a small, dismayed groan escaped her lips.

She was in trouble. Big trouble. Huge trouble. She was infatuated with the man. That had to be the answer.

She wasn't sleeping well and she blamed it on the bed. She'd lost her appetite and cited the change in seasons. She had difficulty concentrating and convinced herself she simply wasn't used to country living after residing in the city for so many years. She told herself a hundred things and more.

Lies.

All lies.

It was Mitch.

"Damn the man!" she swore softly, kicking at a small stone with the toe of her sandal.

"What'd you say, Jessie girl?"

Her head came up. Caught in the act, denial sprang to her lips. "Nothing."

Esther Huckelby was standing on the back stoop, giving a rug from the kitchen a vigorous shake. "Thought I heard you talking to somebody."

Jessie sighed and admitted, "I was."

The housekeeper looked around. Perplexed to find only the two of them, she said: "Who?"

"Myself," she replied with a certain grim amusement.

"Ah—"

It was a very revealing "ah—"

"And just what is *that* supposed to mean?" she grilled the older woman.

"Man trouble," said Esther expertly.

"Man trouble?"

"You can always tell when a woman has a man on her mind."

Jessie was fascinated. She walked toward the house. "How can you tell?"

"Can't sleep. Don't eat right. At sixes and sevens."

"Sounds like the flu to me. Anything else?"

There was a twinkle in the experienced eyes. "Stands around muttering 'damn the man,' instead of doing her chores."

"You heard!"

"I heard." The kitchen rug was given another vigorous shake whether it needed one or not. "Nobody ever said being a woman was easy."

Jessie was in complete agreement. "How true."

"Specially when it comes to a man."

"You can say that again."

Esther Huckelby pursed her lips. "Read somewhere once that you wasn't born a woman, you became one."

"Why, that's very philosophical, Esther."

"Don't know about that," she muttered.

"Where did you read it?"

After some thought, and with a perfectly serious expression on her face, she replied: "Ann Landers."

"I suppose it was also Ann Landers who suggested that the way to a man's heart was through his stomach," Jessie was saying to the housekeeper that same day as Esther Huckelby wrapped up a loaf of freshly baked bread for Mitch.

"Don't think so."

Sometimes Esther had a tendency to take things she said too literally.

Jessie smoothed the skirt of her sundress. "I'm not sure I think this is a good idea."

"You're only being neighborly. Friendly like. I promised Mitch a loaf of my whole-grain bread the next time I baked, and today I baked."

"But you never bake on Mondays. You do the wash on Mondays," Jessie pointed out.

"Never you mind, girl. I'm over twenty-one. I can do as I like." She handed over the warm bread, its wonderful aroma wafting through the entire kitchen, the entire house. "Mitchell Jade is a growing boy. He could use a little mothering, a little kindness."

"Mitch, a growing boy?" she softly hooted.

Esther Huckelby planted both hands on her ample hips, fixed her steadfast gray eyes on the younger woman and dispensed a bit of age-old wisdom: "Every man is still a boy somewheres on the inside. You'd do well to remember that, Jessie. Besides, I seen it in his eyes once."

She was suddenly deadly serious. "What did you see in his eyes?"

"The hurt."

"The hurt?" She failed to understand.

"Mark my words, that one has been hurt and hurt bad." The housekeeper went on, "I had a dog like that. He growled real fierce when anybody got near him. Wasn't mean, though. Not really. Just scared. He'd been kicked so often he just knew he was going to get kicked again."

Jessie fell silent, thinking of what Mitch had confided to her on that first visit to his house. Perhaps one day he would tell her more about it, perhaps not. But Esther was right: he could use a little kindness. Of that, she was certain.

Looping the strap of her leather handbag over her shoulder, she inquired, "Are there any other errands you'd like me to run as long as I'm going to town?"

"Wouldn't mind if you stopped at the five-and-dime to pick me up some more yarn. The color and lot number's there on the counter," said Esther.

"I'll be back by teatime," Jessie called over her shoulder.

DELIVERIES IN REAR read the hand-scribbled note on the front door of Mitch's house.

Jessie glanced down at the loaf of bread in her hand, shrugged her shoulders and followed the sidewalk around to the back of the house.

DOOR UNLOCKED stated the second note. She tried the knob and discovered the door was, indeed, unlocked. Tentatively she opened it and walked into Mitch's kitchen.

In plain view on the tile countertop was a third note. Or series of notes, was more like it. One instructed the delivery man to hang Mitch's clean shirts and pressed pants in the closet and take the check made out for twenty dollars, including tax and tip. Another was a checklist for someone named "Disco" and included mowing the grass and trimming the bushes on the north side of the house. The last requested that the sack of groceries he'd ordered be left on the table and included yet another check.

Jessie set the loaf of homemade bread down and peeked into the brown paper bag. A quick inventory revealed a jar of instant coffee, a can of tomato soup, a box of crackers, two frozen TV dinners just starting to defrost, a loaf of white bread, a quart of milk and a package of cheap chocolate chip cookies.

The professor was no gourmet.

She took it upon herself to put the milk in the refrigerator and the frozen TV dinners in the freezer compartment. He could thank her later. Then she stood in the middle of the huge—and primarily unused—state-of-the-art chrome and glass kitchen, and pondered what to do next.

Perhaps she should simply scribble a note to Mitch, leave the loaf of home-baked bread on the table and make a similarly speedy retreat. It seemed obvious that the man was either out or busy and didn't wish to be disturbed.

Jessie was still trying to make up her mind as to the best course of action to take when she heard it for the first time. Then again and again.

Thud.

Thud. Thud.

It was coming from down below, from the basement, a strange sound, a noise not entirely unlike one wall hitting up against another.

Thud. Thud. Thud.

"What in the world?" Jessie muttered under her breath as she quickly scooted across the kitchen and carefully opened the basement door.

The sound immediately grew louder. There were several more loud thuds in a row, then a grunt or two, perhaps even a moan.

The overhead light was already turned on, and a flight of stairs led downward. Jessie followed it. She turned the corner at the bottom of the steps and there he was: Mitch. She could only stand and stare.

He was dressed in a gray athletic department T-shirt and a pair of sweatpants cut off at mid-thigh. Both were soaked through and clung to his body like a second skin, leaving little of his superb physique to her imagination.

There were thick terry-cloth sweatbands on both wrists and around his forehead. His hair was wet and had darkened to an inky black. His skin glistened. Perspiration beaded on his upper lip and ran down both sides of his face.

He was wearing a particular kind of leather glove on his hands, and, in a series of jabs and punches, he was slamming his fists into a heavy canvas weight. The weight was suspended from one of the steel rafters crisscrossing the basement ceiling. Jessie recognized it as a boxer's punching bag, the type usually found in a gym.

The muscles of his back and shoulders, upper arms, even his thighs stood out in perfect definition. He was in far better shape than she'd realized; he was stronger than she had ever dreamed possible.

But in the end, it was the expression on his face that captured Jessie's attention and held her riveted to the spot at the foot of the stairs. She had never seen it so clearly etched on a set of human features before. Not *hurt*—as Esther claimed to have seen that day—but *hate*. Pure, raw, undiluted hate.

Whatever, whoever, Mitch saw, imagined, thought about, as he threw one ferocious punch after another into the heart of the canvas bag, it was painfully clear what his emotions were: anger and hatred.

Heart pounding, then thundering, Jessie stood there and watched him, mesmerized, horrified. The man fascinated her and he repelled her. He was magnificent and he was hideous. She wanted to run away. She wanted to stay.

It was another minute or two before she heard him muttering, swearing viciously under his breath, calling someone—perhaps himself—a damned fool, a half-wit, a jackass, a bloody bastard, worse.

Against whom was this unabated anger and hate directed? Against himself? Some unseen opponent? His abusive parents? Perhaps even her?

Jessie wanted to reach out and cover her ears: she didn't want to hear any more. She wanted to reach up and cover her eyes: she didn't want to see any more.

This was not the man she knew. This man was a stranger.

Even as tears of reaction sprang into her eyes, she asked herself if a woman could ever really know a man. Could she see into his heart, his heart of darkness, and learn the truth? And when she learned the truth, could she accept it? They were such alien creatures, men.

It was at that instant Mitch seemed to sense he was no longer alone. He stopped and swung around. He saw her. He was stunned.

His breath was coming in great gulps. "Jessie—?"

She couldn't speak, but she knew it was all there in her eyes for him to see: her bewilderment, her repulsion, even her attraction.

She finally managed. "I—the door was unlocked. I just walked in."

An affirmative grunt.

A moment or two passed. "I—I don't understand."

They both knew what she was referring to: not his workout, but his anger.

His chest was rising and falling rapidly. "You don't have to understand. It's got nothing to do with you."

He was wrong, of course. Anything that had to do with him, had to do with her. Even if he didn't see it that way.

Because she had to, she asked, "Why?"

Mitch picked up a towel and began to dry off. He didn't come any nearer to her. "I don't think it's a great mystery. Hitting a punching bag is a good way to vent frustrations. A workout makes me feel better mentally and physically." He tossed the used towel into a laundry basket beside the washer and dryer on the side wall. "What are you doing here, anyway?"

"Bread."

"Bread?"

"Esther baked this morning. She sent me over with a loaf of homemade bread. Said she promised."

A half smile. "So she did. I'd almost forgotten."

"She didn't."

He picked up a second towel—there was a stack of them on top of the dryer—and began to mop at his face and hair before he commented, "Obviously not."

A sort of brittle calm came over her. "I put the milk and frozen food away."

"Thanks."

"You're welcome."

There was something to be said for mundane conversation, Jessie decided, as she shifted her weight from one foot to the other. It was far easier to talk about Esther and her bread, about putting his melting groceries away, than it was to blurt out: This is the right time and the right place... but are you the *right* man?

Chances were, Mitch didn't know, himself.

They both started to speak at once.

"Go ahead," he said.

"No, you first," she countered.

He wrapped the towel around his neck and held onto each end with a large hand. "I was just going to ask if you'd like a cold drink."

There wasn't anything funny about the situation she found herself in. It was, perhaps, only a little ridiculous. Jessie nearly laughed. "A cold drink?"

"I've got some Gatorade." He paused, and a frown furrowed his forehead. "I could make a glass of ice coffee for you, if you'd prefer that."

"Neither, thank you."

The dark brows drew together again. "I know what I'd like to do."

She was almost afraid to ask. "What's that?"

"I'd like to kiss you—" Mitch glanced down at his sweat-soaked body "—but under the circumstances I don't think you would like it." He smiled at her boldly. "But if you're willing to wait a few minutes I can be in and out of the shower in record time."

He was flirting with her. She'd never known what to do with a flirting male. She'd never understood how she was supposed to respond to a double entendre, a sly, witty suggestion, a sexual innuendo. Maybe it was something you learned in high school, and she'd been absent that day.

"I—I'm sorry. I can't wait. I have other errands to run, and I promised Esther and my grandmother that I would be home in time for tea."

The humor and a lot more faded from his eyes. Then he shrugged his massive shoulders and said nonchalantly, "It was just an idea."

Jessie glanced down at her watch. "In fact, I'd better be going. It's later than I thought." She set one foot on the bottom stair.

Mitch took a step toward her. The shadows in the basement seemed to close around them. "Running away isn't going to change anything, Jessie."

She felt the heat creep up her neck and onto her cheeks. "I'm not running away."

They were softly spoken but an edge of steel underlined each word. "Yes, you are. You may as well face it right now. I am what I am. You are what you are."

"I know," she said, eyes downcast.

"Don't hate me for it."

Her head flew up. "Hate you for it? Dear God, Mitch, I don't hate you. I could never hate you."

There was something in his eyes. "Never is a long, long time, sweetheart."

She closed her mouth and found herself staring at him. "I could *never* hate you," she repeated with every ounce of conviction in her body.

She stopped short of saying I love you. It was the wrong time and place for a declaration of that kind.

And it was *far* later than she had thought, Jessie realized as she left his house that day, for somewhere, somehow, without her consent or permission, she seemed to have fallen in love with Mitchell Jade.

Chapter Nine

Look Homeward, Angel

"I'm too heavy for you to carry all the way up the hill to the Golden Raintree," Christine protested.

Mitch glanced down at the slender woman sitting on the kitchen chair. "You're not too heavy. You're just a little slip of a thing," he teased affectionately. "Besides, I can always stop and rest if I have to."

In spite of her failing health, Christine Brick Warren's blue eyes sparkled; each pale cheek had a spot of pink in the center. "I must confess I'm excited," she said, clapping her wrinkled hands together with glee. "I can't remember the last time I went on a picnic."

"Then it's been too long," he said.

She fussed with the lightweight cotton shawl on her lap. "I suppose James would have taken me if I had asked, or if he'd been in better health that last summer before he died." She gazed up at him. "Are you sure you don't mind doing this?"

"I don't mind, Christine." Mitch's mouth softened. "I did promise, after all."

Patting his arm, she said, "I know you did, my boy. I know you did."

Neither of them mentioned that the picnic had originally been scheduled for the middle of July when the great sprawling Raintree atop the hill would be in full flower. It was only nearing the end of May, but it was apparent to everyone that Christine would not live to see the Golden Raintree in bloom again.

Mitch went on. "Jessie has been busy all morning preparing for our picnic. We wouldn't want to disappoint her, would we?"

"No, we wouldn't."

He smiled at her. "She's had me make at least a half-dozen trips up that darn hill already, hauling quilts, your wheelchair, *two* picnic baskets, even a can of bug spray in case the ants decide to crash our party."

The corners of Christine's mouth turned up. "My granddaughter is a very organized woman."

Mitch chuckled. "I'm discovering that for myself."

"Apparently the hard way this morning," she said. "I suppose it's one of the reasons she's such a successful businessowner."

He agreed. "Believe me, I wouldn't want Jessie to be any other way. I like her just as she is."

Her grandmother gave a satisfied nod of her silvery head and deftly changed the subject. "What are we having for lunch today?"

"Oh, no, you don't. I'm not going to give away any of Jessie's and Esther's surprises." He made a zipper-motion across his mouth. "My lips are sealed."

She sighed. "Then I don't suppose there's any sense in offering you a bribe."

"None whatsoever." His curiosity overcame him. "What kind of bribe?"

"Peppermint sticks," came the ready answer.

"How many?"

"Half a bag."

His dark eyebrows arched. "It's tempting, but..."

She upped the ante. "A whole bag."

"Jessie will have my head if I blab," Mitch muttered under his breath. Still, he decided it wouldn't, couldn't, hurt to tell Christine a little. "Let's just say we're having some of your favorites."

But that was *all* he would say on the subject.

"I'm ready whenever you are," she prompted.

"You keep that shawl around your shoulders in case you feel a chill," Mitch admonished.

"I'm not going to feel any chill. There isn't a hint of a breeze outside. In fact, it's rather warm for this time of year. You and Jessie couldn't have picked a better day."

He gathered Christine's frail form up in his arms. "Try to clasp your hands behind my neck." She did as he suggested. "Are you comfortable?"

"Perfectly. I feel like the Queen of Sheba being carried around by such a strong, handsome man."

"Flattery will get you nowhere. I'm still not going to tell you what we're having for lunch."

Innocent eyes were turned on him. "Did I ask you to?"

Mitch gave the elderly woman a charming smile in response. "You were hinting, definitely hinting."

With his passenger securely ensconced in his arms, he elbowed the screen door open and stepped out onto the back stoop.

"It is a beautiful day," came her sweet alto.

He took a deep breath. "It is, indeed."

They started across the barnyard and up the hill. The sky was blue on blue with only a wisp of white clouds high overhead. It had rained briefly the day before, making the ground soft and green beneath Mitch's feet. Winter was gone from the land, and everywhere the earth was coming to life again. It was spring: a time of rebirth, the season of renewal.

Unaware that she spoke aloud Christine murmured, "'Oh, how my heart yearns for the sight of thee. I'm coming home. I will be home in the spring.'"

Mitch glanced down at her. "I'm sorry. I didn't hear you. I must have been daydreaming. What did you say?"

A secret smile graced her lips. "It's nothing, my dear. Just something my grandmother once wrote in a letter a long, long time ago."

"You've had some amazing women in your family," he observed.

"Yes, we have."

"What is it about them, do you think?" Mitch asked.

She gave his question serious consideration before answering. "I believe it's because each of them was a true Quaker, a woman of love and peace. Yet each had to confront some form of violence that threatened to destroy all that she had, all that she believed in, all that she was. Elizabeth Banks, Mary Long Sutter, my own mother—"

"—and yourself."

Christine bowed to his judgment. "Myself, my daughter—" her voice choked for a moment "—my beloved Jessie. There has been an unbreakable bond between the women of my family for generations, a bond that sometimes defies the limitations of time and place."

Mitch wasn't sure he understood. He asked her to elaborate and she did.

"Each of us has been a reflection of the historical period in which she lived. Elizabeth Banks migrated to Indiana during the early settlement of the Heartland.

Mary Long Sutter traveled to Oregon by wagon train in 1849. My mother grew up in the era of the Civil War and Reconstruction. I lived through the Great War. My daughter, World War II. Even Jessie has seen far too much horror and violence in her young life. We've had to learn how to be strong, how to endure the loss of parents, children, husbands.'' Her voice grew gentle. "We each loved one man above all else but God. And we seemed to possess a special gift."

"A special gift?"

"A certain sensibility, then."

With Christine in his arms, Mitch kept climbing up the hill toward the Golden Raintree and the chestnut-haired woman waiting there for them. "Jessie told you about the figure she saw in Popplewell's, didn't she?"

"Yes."

"It sounds crazy."

"It does, indeed."

He crooked a brow at her. "But you don't think it is crazy, do you?"

"No."

He was riddled with curiosity. "Why not?"

She took so long to answer that he wasn't sure she had heard him.

Finally Christine said, "Because it happened to me very much in the same way."

That was the last thing he'd expected her to say. "I— I don't think I understand."

"It's possible you never will. My dear James tried, bless his soul, but I don't think he ever really did."

Mitch was confused. He blew out his breath and mumbled, "Yeah, well, for that matter, what man does understand a woman?"

The smile Christine bestowed upon him was beatific. "It isn't necessary for you to understand Jessie's 'gift.' Just love her, Mitch. Just love her."

His face was close to hers; he could feel her pure blue eyes fixed on him. A moment passed. "I do love her."

Another moment went by.

"Have you told her?"

He frowned. "Not yet."

"Don't wait too long."

"I won't."

"She is going to need you—your strength, your compassion, your love."

Mitch tried to swallow and found his throat was constricted with emotion. "I—I know."

"She's going to need you soon. Very soon. I haven't much longer to live."

No hysteria. No melodrama. It was simply a statement of fact.

Mitch thought he saw a fleeting moment of sadness on the aging face. But there was primarily a kind of quiet acceptance of the inevitable. He recalled what the dear old woman in his arms had told him about the Society of Friends and the principles upon which it had been founded. The greatest of these, she had said, were simplicity, peace and serenity.

Mitch looked down at the fragile figure he was carrying up the hill. Christine Brick Warren was going to be a true Quaker woman until the end.

His passenger apparently decided to change the subject. She studied the circles under his eyes for a minute or so, and then commented, "You look tired, Mitch. Have you been sleeping well the past several weeks?"

He shrugged. "You know how it is at the end of the school year with final exams and grades and the summer coming up."

"A busy time."

"A very busy time."

"You've had a lot on your mind."

He nodded. "I have some important decisions to make."

She didn't bandy words with him. "Will you go, or will you stay?"

The smile he gave her was slightly sardonic. "Sometimes I think you can read my mind."

"I'm no mind reader, Mitch. I'm merely ninety-one years old. A certain amount of insight seems to come with age."

"If I lived to be one hundred and ninety, I would never have your gift to see into the human heart."

A flush of self-conscious pink washed over her face. "We Friends believe that each man and woman of us must look within and try to find the truth of what we should do." She leaned toward him and pressed her lips against his cheek for a moment. "You are a good man, Mitchell Jade. I know you will do what is right."

Even as she spoke, Mitch realized that he would never forget Christine's words. And, until the end of his days, he remembered the sweet kiss she bestowed upon him that afternoon.

"We're nearly there," he said to her as they approached the summit of the hill behind the old farmhouse. "I see Jessie waiting for us."

SHE WATCHED AS MITCH came out the back door of the farmhouse with her grandmother cradled in his arms. They started toward her, following the path she had already taken a dozen times herself that day: across the barnyard, through the meadow and up the hill.

From where she stood beneath the shade of the Golden Raintree Jessie would see the entire panorama of the surrounding countryside—the rich, dark fields, now plowed and planted for spring, a herd of grazing dairy cows, the winding road to town, and there, there in the distance was the Happy Valley.

If she turned and looked in the opposite direction she could make out the stone fence marking the boundaries of the family cemetery, a cluster of red barns and beyond, the Great Wood.

They came nearer and she went to greet them. "Hello, you two. I was wondering when you'd get here."

"We were enjoying the walk," volunteered Mitch.

"Or the ride, in my case," said her grandmother. "It's the first time I've been carried up this hill, and I must confess I rather liked it."

Mitch carefully settled his charge in the waiting wheelchair. "How's that, Christine?"

"Fine. Thank you, my dear. I can't imagine how you managed the whole business without even getting out of breath."

He grinned down at her. "There's no need to flatter me now, we'll soon be unveiling the food Jessie and Esther packed for our picnic."

"What a perfectly splendid day for a picnic, too," Christine said to her granddaughter.

Jessie put her head back and gazed up at the sky. "We lucked out with the weather, that's for sure."

Mitch came up and stood shoulder to shoulder with her, and they gazed out over the lush green valley. "This is mighty pretty country. I can see why Elizabeth and Joshua Banks picked this piece of land to settle.''

"Speaking of Elizabeth and Joshua—'' Christine patted the breast pocket of her cotton dress and acted very pleased with herself ''—I have something to give you, Jessie, after we've had lunch.''

Her curiosity was aroused. "In that case, let's eat.''

"Good. I'm famished,'' declared Mitch, rubbing his hands together in anticipation.

Jessie positioned her grandmother's wheelchair in the shade of the Golden Raintree, and then, with Mitch's help, spread a waterproof tarpaulin out on the ground at their feet. A colorful patchwork quilt followed.

"You sure we ought to use an antique quilt?'' queried Mitch as he straightened the corners on his side.

Jessie reassured him it was quite all right. "For one thing it isn't an antique.''

His brow creased. "Looks old to me.''

"As a matter of fact, it's brand new. It only *looks* old.'' She went down on her haunches and opened the first of the two wicker picnic baskets. "The material has been tea dyed to appear antique,'' she explained. "A common enough practice, I suppose, among some quilters. This one was made last winter for Grandmama by Becky Sue Stoots.''

The name seemed to ring a bell with Mitch. "She's the young woman who's pregnant, isn't she?''

"That's the one.'' She quickly and efficiently removed plates, knives and forks, glassware, napkins and the like, and laid three places for lunch.

"Jessie came to me several weeks ago with an idea about how we might help Becky Sue and Lyman,'' her grandmother expounded. "We're trying to encourage the girl to market her needlework through some of the local craft shops."

"Becky Sue is very talented. She only lacks motivation and self-confidence. We're hoping to change that."

That was Jessie's final word on the subject. She had more important things to see to on this particular day.

As the platters of food were uncovered and placed out on the quilt, Christine exclaimed in an excited voice: "Fried chicken, homemade bread, pickles, corn relish, freshly baked peach pie. Lemonade and iced tea to drink." Tears sprang to her eyes. "Jessie, you remembered—"

She gave the wrinkled hand a squeeze. "Of course I remembered, Grandmama."

"It's just like the picnic we had along the banks of No Name Creek on that last glorious day of summer and sun, July 1917," came the nostalgic whisper. "Except they're all gone now: James, Charlie and Hannah, Louise. I'm the only one still here." She reached up and brushed her cheek with the back of her hand. "Not that it's any reason for me to get all teary. I have you two and no one could be happier."

Jessie gently suggested, "Let me fix you a plate of food. What would you like to start with?"

A shaky finger pointed at the dish piled high with fried chicken. "That drumstick looks pretty good."

She speared the drumstick with a fork and added a helping of potato salad and corn relish before setting the plate on her grandmother's lap. Later she would notice that the food had only been picked at.

There was certainly nothing wrong with Mitch's appetite, however. He managed to eat half of the chicken and most of the peach pie by himself.

After his third glass of lemonade, he lay back on the quilt and sighed contentedly. "Best fried chicken I've ever had. Best peach pie, too."

"Esther will be pleased."

"You're pleased, too, Jessie," said Christine. "I know for a fact that you made the pies yourself."

She looked up from where she sat, feet tucked demurely beneath her. "How do you know that?"

Blue eyes twinkled mischievously. "I have my ways."

Jessie arched one eyebrow and speculated: "A little mouse in the kitchen corner?"

Her grandmother sniffed. "I'm afraid I'm not at liberty to divulge my sources."

That made her laugh out loud. "In other words, Esther told you."

"She simply said that you'd come a long way as a cook this spring under her expert tutelage."

"Under her expert tutelage?"

"Well, I believe her exact words were, 'That Jessie girl could be a passably good cook if she had half a mind to.'"

"That is a compliment coming from Esther Huckelby." Jessie let Mitch in on the joke. "It's well-known that Esther considers herself the best cook in three counties."

"The *only* cook," amended Christine.

"In that case, remind me to be extra nice to the woman." He gave another contented sigh. "I can certainly vouch for her whole-grain bread, and her chicken."

The mention of whole-grain bread brought back that Monday in his basement. Jessie didn't want to think about it, not right now. This was to be her grandmother's special day. She turned back to the figure in the wheelchair. "Don't keep me in suspense a moment longer, Grandmama. You said something about Elizabeth and Joshua before lunch. What is it?"

Christine reached into her dress pocket and removed a small leather pouch. She held it out to Jessie. "My parents gave me this on my eighteenth birthday. I have always treasured it. Now it is part of the legacy that I pass on to you."

Jessie took the small parcel from the aged hands and undid the fastenings on the front. Reverently she removed the object inside. It was a tiny portrait of a young woman painted on an oval-shaped piece of ivory.

In a hushed tone, she said, "It's Elizabeth, isn't it?"

"Yes, this is Elizabeth, your great-great-great-grandmother. She was twenty years old and a recent bride at the time the miniature was done. I believe you will find mention of it in her journal."

Jessie handed the tiny portrait to Mitch. Then she took the leather-bound volume that she had brought with her at her grandmother's request and opened to a page toward the beginning. She read aloud:

April 19, 1821

On this day we did reach Cincinnati and meet up with a man named John James Audubon, who offered to paint my portrait and a miniature for the sum of two dollars. I thought it unseemly, but Joshua insisted. "Thee knows it would make happy me, Elizabeth. Thy portrait will be the first thing we place in our new home."

April 24, 1821

Joshua is pleased with the portrait done by Mr.

Audubon. He paid the Gentleman three dollars
and we bid him "Adieu" this very morning, since
it is time we traveled upriver. We hear the Land is
rich in Indiana and we grow anxious to reach our
new Home.

"She has your eyes, Jessie," came the improbable
observation from the man sitting beside her on the quilt.
"Or should I say that *you* have hers?" Mitch shook his
head in puzzlement and mumbled under his breath,
"Maybe that's where I've seen that unusual shade of
brown before."

Jessie paid him no heed; she had other things on her
mind. "I wonder what happened to the portrait."

Mitch's head came up. "The portrait?"

"It says right here in Elizabeth's journal that Audubon offered to paint her portrait and a miniature for
two dollars. We have the miniature, but what happened to the portrait?" She looked up at her grandmother. "Do you have any idea?"

"I don't know. I don't believe that I've ever heard
anyone in the family talk about the existence of a portrait. It must have been lost a long time ago."

"Lost a long time ago—" repeated Jessie thoughtfully. She brought her attention back to the present.
"Thank you, Grandmama. I will treasure the miniature always."

A quivering hand reached out to gently cup her chin.
"And someday you will have a daughter and a granddaughter and perhaps even a great-granddaughter to
show the miniature to and you will tell the story of
Elizabeth Banks and all of us who came after her."

Jessie tried to speak and found she had no voice. She sank her teeth into her bottom lip to stop her mouth from trembling.

Christine cleared her throat. "Come, give me a kiss, my dear, and then make Mitch take you for a walk. I believe I will have my afternoon nap right here beneath the Golden Raintree."

"As you wish, Grandmama." She stood, bent over the figure in the wheelchair and pressed her lips to the cool cheek. Then, in a hoarse whisper: "I love you."

"And I love you, Jessie. I will always be with you. Remember that," came the whispered assurance.

"ARE YOU ALL RIGHT?" inquired Mitch as he reached for her hand.

Jessie took in a deep breath and let it out again. "I will be."

Side by side they walked along the path that led from the hilltop to the high meadow and beyond to the family cemetery. Neither spoke until they had gone some distance. Then Jessie sat down on a large boulder and stretched her legs out in front of her.

"I've been reading more about Elizabeth and Joshua," she told him. "And Nathaniel Currant."

Mitch propped one booted foot up on the rocks and rested his forearm on his thigh. "What have you found out?"

"A lot about daily life on the frontier for one thing. The section I read last night had to do with bee-hunting and gathering honey."

"How edifying."

"I've learned how the pioneers treated fevers and what Elizabeth calls *ague* or the 'shakes.' Apparently they believed it was brought on by drinking foul water or breathing impure air."

"Breathing impure air?"

"She had it on the best authority. Major Currant claimed considerable experience with fevers and such from the time when he served under General Jackson."

"Any more about the eternal triangle?"

She took the journal from the oversize pocket of her skirt. "Perhaps you should judge that for yourself."

Mitch sat down beside her on the huge rock. "I have a better idea. Why don't you tell me what you've read?"

Jessie opened the leather book to the page she had marked the evening before, but instead of looking down, she looked out toward the horizon. "Elizabeth writes about Joshua going off to have their harvest ground into cornmeal and Nathaniel staying behind to stand guard."

"So, the husband rides off and leaves the opportunity wide open for the other man."

"Perhaps. I did notice that in this part of the diary Elizabeth begins by writing about Major Currant and by the end of the week she's referring to him as Nathaniel."

"Just goes to prove my point."

"Which point is that?"

"The point about the eternal triangle—two men and one woman. It's always bound to bring trouble." Adding as an afterthought, "A woman so frequently does."

"Are you saying that letting a woman in your life is bound to bring you trouble?"

"Now, Jessie, that's not what I said."

"It's what you implied."

"Don't go getting emotional on me, honey."

She swallowed and told him, "It's been an emotional day for me. Earlier this morning I found my grandmother reading the very Bible verse that Elizabeth mentions in her journal." She thumbed to the entry and read. "'Yea, though I walk through the valley of the shadow of death, I will fear no evil: for thou art with me; thy rod and thy staff they comfort me.'

"After I found my grandmother reading that verse, she advised me of the plans for her funeral and burial."

He swore softly. "God, I'm sorry, honey."

She shook her head. "I know it's something that has to be dealt with. I tried to be brave for her sake and my own. But, Mitch, I can't bear the thought of losing her."

He brought her closer to him and slipped a comforting arm around her shoulders. "I know. Neither can I."

Some minutes later Jessie was able to continue. "She told me that she wants to be buried with the others."

"The others?"

A gesture directed toward the walled area ahead of them. "She said, 'Put me with Mama and Papa, dear Charlie, Hannah, and my own beloved James.'" Her voice cracked again. "They're all there, you see. Elizabeth. Joshua. The old woman she knew as Grandmother. Her parents. Her brothers and sisters. Most of all, my grandfather."

Mitch stopped and drew her into his arms. He was so solid and so wonderful. She dropped her head to his chest and pressed her face into the clean-smelling cotton of his shirt. She could hear the strong, steady rhythm of his heartbeat. The heat of his body emanated from him and cloaked her in a soothing warmth. His touch was understanding and comforting.

She raised her head and looked up at him. "I don't know what I would have done without you these past few weeks. Thank you, Mitch."

"There's no need to thank me, Jessie," he said, his voice a throaty rumble. "I wish I could do more."

"It was very sweet of you to help me arrange the picnic for Grandmama. I know it was the right thing to do."

"I did it for Christine because I care about her."

Jessie could feel the increased rate of his heartbeat beneath her fingertips.

His eyes were a shade of green she had never seen before. There was a vulnerability there he had never previously revealed to her. He took her face in his hands. "I did it for you, too, Jessie, because I care about you."

She had thought it would take courage to reveal what was in her heart. She had planned to keep it a secret, her secret, for as long as she could. *I care about you*: it was a beginning. She would tell him a little, perhaps, of what was in her own heart. A smile started across her face, then became a grin and ended with a happy burst of laughter. "And I care for you, Mitch, I really do."

CHRISTINE HEARD the delighted laughter from her granddaughter and opened her eyes. She watched for a moment as Jessie threw her arms around Mitchell Jade's neck and kissed him squarely on the mouth.

"So Mitch finally decided to tell Jessie something that has made her happy," she murmured with a pleased smile as her eyes drifted shut again.

"Is he a good man?" came the question.

"I believe that he is," she said, unsure if she spoke aloud or if the answer was merely an echo in her own mind.

*"Will he love her and cherish her and hold her close
to him all the days of his life, as I loved and cherished
you, as I held you close to me all the days of my life?"*

"I hope so. I pray so."

Christine opened her eyes. She could feel the wind,
the glorious wind in her hair and face. She was feeling
surprisingly young and strong, vital and healthy. She
wanted to run through the meadow and up the hill and
wrap her arms around the thick trunk of the great tree,
to feel its bark press into her flesh, to be alive, truly alive
as she had not been in years.

Out of the corner of one eye she saw a flash of color
in the afternoon sunlight. How odd. She hadn't thought
the Golden Raintree was in bloom. She wanted suddenly to walk beneath its cooling shade and feel its
shower of brilliant golden-yellow blossoms on her skin.
She opened her arms wide and ran toward the tree.

"Christine."

She thought she heard someone call her name. She
turned and raised a hand to shield her eyes from the
sun's glare as she searched the horizon.

Where? Yes, there! There was something, someone,
coming toward her. She could see clearly now. She
watched as a young man climbed up her hill; there was
a bouquet of blue flowers in his hand. Periwinkles.

She knew it was James.

Joy filled her heart to bursting. She raised a hand
high in the air and waved to him. In turn, his was raised
in greeting. Then he was running to her and he swept
her up in his arms.

She wanted to laugh and cry at the same time. It had
been so long, so terribly long, since she had felt his arms
around her, holding her tight, holding her for dear life.

"James—" She had forgotten how young and how handsome he was.

"Christine, my own sweet girl, my only love," he murmured before he kissed her.

She didn't understand. What was James doing here? And he was young again, not old. She was young again. Young and pretty and all new.

She must be dreaming. That was it, it must be a dream. If so, she knew she never wanted to awaken.

"What are you doing here?" she finally asked James.

His eyes were the same color of hazel with flecks of green and yellow. *"I promised I would always come for you, my love."*

She nodded. "And I promised to always be here waiting for you."

James smiled at her and then declared, *"We climbed this hill so many times during our lives and stood beneath this Golden Raintree."*

She joined in. "We shook the branches until the yellow blossoms rained down on our faces."

"We caught them in our outstretched hands."

"Golden Rain."

"You remembered," murmured James.

Christine's love for him shone in her eyes. She understood at last. *"I remembered, beloved. I always have."*

Then they joined hands and walked toward Home together. . . .

Chapter Ten

The Final Home

Silence.

There was only silence in the white frame meeting-house. Silence stretching out to fill minute after minute. Rows of silent men and women, sitting, waiting.

Cap in hand, a grizzled old man struggled to his feet. He took a carefully pressed white cotton handkerchief from his pocket and wiped at his mouth. Then he cleared his throat and began: "Don't rightly know how this works. Not a Quaker myself."

A gentle voice from the back of the room reassured him, "We are all Friends here."

The old man shifted his weight from one foot to the other. It wasn't often he spoke out in public. "Back during the Great Depression I was out of work, like lots of folks, and I couldn't feed my family, let alone buy my oldest boy shoes for school." A muscle in his face began to twitch. "Thing is, we woke up one morning and there on our doorstep was a bushel basket of vegetables and three loaves of homemade bread, still warm from the oven. Next to them was a pair of farmer's boots. They wasn't new, mind you, but somebody had cleaned them up real nice."

He stopped to catch his breath.

A page rustled as it was turned. Someone coughed. Through an open window, the soft June breeze entered the small church in the wood. The sound of buzzing insects could be discerned in the bushes outside, the faraway lowing of a herd of cattle.

But in this place there was only a sense of simplicity, peace and serenity. As there had been since 1836 when the first Friends in Henry County built this meeting-house with their own hands.

The old man was ready to resume his story. "My oldest son wore those boots to school for the next two years and his brother after him. We never did know for sure where they come from." He rubbed his chin. "But I always 'spected it was Mrs. Warren, and that's why I'm here today to pay my respects and say 'thank you, ma'am.'" He nodded his head once, twice, and slowly sat down.

Silence.

A clear young voice recited: "'Blessed are the merciful: for they shall obtain mercy. Blessed are the pure in heart: for they shall see God.'"

Another added, "'Blessed are they that mourn: for they shall be comforted.'"

Jessie sat quietly among her grandmother's friends and neighbors, *her* friends and neighbors, and tried to take comfort from their words. She waited, as they all did, for God to speak through one of them. For it was a special time of remembering, a time to keep silence, and a time for speaking of Christine Brick Warren with love and affection.

A little girl of six or seven stood and blurted out: "I liked the lady. She had pretty blue eyes and she laughed a lot and she always gave me a peppermint stick."

Jessie felt a smile tug at her mouth. There was a tender muted laugh here and there.

It was some time before the gruff familiar voice of Esther Huckelby said from the other side of the small meetinghouse: "Not so long ago Christine had me read to her from the book of Ecclesiastes about there being 'a time to plant, and a time to pluck up that which is planted.' I promised her then that she'd have her garden this year, come what may. And I intend to keep that promise."

Jessie felt sudden tears sting her eyes. Poor Esther. She had taken it hard. Real hard. She hadn't been herself for the past week.

But then who had?

There was silence once again.

The next to rise to the occasion was Professor Ratcliff. He solemnly faced the congregation of men and women. The distinguished gray-haired academician opened his mouth to speak and nothing came out.

He swallowed hard and tried a second time. "There have been two women who've changed the course of my life. My loving wife, Dorothy—" he reached down and grasped the hand of the pleasant looking brunette seated beside him "—and Christine Warren. I would never have met the first without the latter.

"Forty years ago I had a burning desire to go to college and become a teacher. It was right after the Second World War and I didn't have the money for books or tuition, and jobs were scarce. A certain Quaker lady made me a loan. There were only two conditions. I wasn't to tell anyone as long as she was living, and I was to pay her back by helping out another needy student. I have tried to live up to those conditions.

"I won't kid you or myself. I will miss...Christine."
His deep baritone broke as he uttered her name, and he
sat down and bowed his head. His wife reached over
and placed her hand on his shoulder.

Five minutes passed.

Ten.

Fifteen.

From across the way, through the silence of the summer day, came a contralto singing the hymn, "Amazing Grace." It was from the First Methodist Church just
down the road. They all sat and listened; somehow it
seemed fitting that they do so.

At their founding, the Quakers—the Society of
Friends—had adopted no formal religious beliefs, no
rituals, no sacraments. There had been no pastors in
their meetinghouses, no set service of worship, no
hymns. It had been their custom to sit and wait for God
to speak through one of their members.

In crossing the continents and in the centuries since,
much of that had changed, and yet there were those
who preferred the old ways and the old customs. There
were those who still sat in "silence" and waited.

It was some time before a middle-aged matron in the
back of the room offered: "I've known Christine for
nearly thirty years. I don't expect I'll see her like again
in my lifetime."

Another contributed: "She was a good friend."

Yet another: "She was a Friend in the truest sense of
the word."

A self-conscious Becky Sue Stoots, her stomach
rounded with pregnancy, said in a whisper: "I wish I
could be more like her. I'm going to try."

Then silence reigned in the hall.

At last Mitchell Jade unfolded his six-foot three-inch frame and stood, towering over the assemblage.

Jessie's heart began to pick up speed until it was thundering in her breast. She knew how difficult this had to be for Mitch. His skin was drawn tightly over his cheekbones; it was tinged an unhealthy shade of gray. The lines on his face were marked. He looked ten years older than the last time she had seen him.

When he spoke his voice filled the room. "I knew Christine for only a few short months. Yet I loved her and I believe that she loved me. For the rest of my life I will miss her more than I can say."

The silence was deafening.

Mitch abruptly sat down and turned his face to the wall.

Jessie realized she'd been holding her breath all the while he was speaking. She exhaled tremulously and wiped the tears from her cheeks.

She tried to calm herself. She sat quietly and closed her eyes, determined to absorb the peace and the serenity of this place.

She remembered the first time she'd spoken out in Meeting. She couldn't have been more than eight or nine years old, a solemn little girl with huge eyes and gangly legs and French braids that hung halfway down her back.

For some reason she'd been wearing her favorite dress on that particular Sunday morning: periwinkle blue with little pink rosebuds on the collar.

The meetinghouse was filled with mostly older folks like her grandparents; her mother and father attended the church in town. This was a traditional "silent" meeting. What seemed like hours had passed and no one had said a word.

Jessie had stared out the window until every leaf on every tree was indelibly etched on her memory. She had watched Mrs. Trueblood reading her Bible and Mr. Trueblood dozing beside her. Now and again, the woman gave him a nudge with her elbow. She had counted the wooden planks in the floor and had straightened the skirt of her dress umpteen times.

Then she had turned her head and gazed at her grandmother sitting beside her, and suddenly her heart was filled to overflowing with love for the sweet, gentle creature she had always called Grandmama.

The next thing Jessie knew, she was on her feet. "I love my grandma most of all," she declared.

She'd quickly sat down again, her young face burning bright red with embarrassment. She had wanted to get up and run far, far away as fast as she could. But she hadn't, of course.

Christine Brick Warren had reached out and taken her granddaughter's hand, then, and had held it lovingly in hers until one by one the members had silently risen to their feet and filed out the meetinghouse door.

Jessie rose to her feet now.

"The first time I spoke in this meetinghouse I was no more than eight or nine years old. Some of you may recall that day." She smiled at old Mrs. Trueblood, Mr. Trueblood having passed on some years before. "I stood here and I declared to the entire Meeting 'I love my grandma most of all.' That was true when I was a child. It is still true today. I love my grandmother most of all."

Jessie watched as Mitch slowly turned in his seat and fixed his eyes on her.

She was intensely aware of him as she continued. "I loved my grandfather most of all, too. Folks around here often said there was something different, something special about my grandparents, as if they had a secret and weren't going to share it with anybody else." She paused. "There was no great secret. James and Christine Warren were willing to share it in a hundred ways every day, and they did."

It was so quiet she could have heard a pin drop.

"It was love."

Mitch gave her an encouraging, if watery, smile.

Jessie brushed away an unself-conscious tear and took in a fortifying breath. "Whenever I feel sad and a little lonely—and I often do these days—I remind myself that Grandmama is with Grandfather now, and there is no place in heaven or on earth that she would rather be. Somehow I know that these two dear, wonderful people are together again, and I cannot despair."

She took her seat.

From the doorway of the meetinghouse the words of a sonorous voice came in benediction: "'The Lord bless thee, and keep thee. The Lord make His face shine upon thee, and be gracious unto thee. The Lord lift up His countenance upon thee, and give thee peace. Now and forevermore.'"

In unison: "Amen."

"Amen," whispered Jessie as she rose to take her final leave.

Her heart, at least for a time, was at peace.

"IT WAS GOOD of you to supervise the reception, Esther, and all of the serving, and the cleanup. I don't know what I would have done without you," Jessie was saying to the housekeeper as they stood in the middle of the large farmhouse kitchen. Most of the funeral guests had departed, and they were taking stock of the leftovers. She passed a weary hand over her eyes. "What in the world are we going to do with all this donated food?"

"I venture to say you won't feel much like cooking for a while, Jessie girl, and you've got to eat something. You look skinnier than ever to me."

She heaved a sigh. "But there's enough here to feed an army."

Esther Huckelby took a damp dishcloth and began to wipe off the countertops as had been her custom after meals in this house for the past eight years. "That Mitchell Jade eats enough for an army."

"Even Mitch couldn't make a dent in this mountain of food before it would start to spoil. You'll take some home with you, won't you?"

The housekeeper dried her hands on a kitchen towel, folded it neatly into thirds, and hung it over a rack under the sink. "If you insist."

"I insist."

Esther planted her hands on her hips and said in a characteristic burst of frankness: "I do know a few folks that have fallen on hard times—"

Jessie made a gesture toward the refrigerator, the cupboards, the walk-in pantry, all filled to overflowing in the past few days. Her grandmother had helped so many people over the years. Now it seemed that each and every one of them was determined to repay her kindness and generosity by bringing a covered dish, a tin of meat, a plate of homemade cookies, sometimes a pie or a cake, as well. "Please take whatever you think you can give away."

"Well, now, there's the Ketchum family lives down by Big Blue River. They got a houseful of little ones and I heard tell Mr. Ketchum lost his job at the furniture factory last week."

Jessie nodded sympathetically. "Better take a twenty-dollar bill out of Grandmama's cookie jar, too. They may need cash to buy milk." She reached behind her and tried to massage the tension from her shoulders. "Let's send that canned ham, a cake and several of those casseroles over to the Stoots, while we're at it."

"Gossip says they're having a hard time."

"I'm afraid it may be true. I haven't talked to Becky Sue about selling her needlework on consignment at some of the local shops since Grandmama died. But I'll see to it soon."

"First thing you got to do is take care of yourself, Jessie girl. You're plumb wore out. Christine would never forgive me if I didn't look after you proper." She clicked her tongue in disapproval. "Maybe I should stay the night."

Jessie slipped an arm around the older woman's waist. "I appreciate the concern and the offer, but I know how anxious you've been to live in your own home again. Now you can." She gave her a reassuring hug. "I'll be all right."

"If you're sure—"

"I'm sure."

Esther glanced back over her shoulder. "Anybody still in the parlor?"

"Just Dorothy and Richard Ratcliff. Mitch went out to get a breath of fresh air. I think he's back by the barn."

The housekeeper frowned in consternation. "He's taking it real hard, that one."

Jessie stared out the kitchen window in the direction of the barnyard. "Yes, I know he is."

"Not that we all don't miss Christine." Esther sniffed and wiped her eyes with the corner of her apron.

She chewed on her bottom lip and said wistfully: "Sometimes I'll walk down the hallway to Grandmama's bedroom, half expecting to find her there, pillows propped up behind her back, poring over one of her photograph albums or a bunch of old letters."

Esther stood there. "House feels different."

"It does."

"Seems mighty quiet."

"It is."

The older woman took another swipe at her face. "Guess I'd better get a move on if I'm going to deliver all this food before dark."

"I'll help carry the bags to your car," volunteered Jessie.

Before she drove off down the country road, Esther Huckelby made it clear to her: "I'll be over tomorrow afternoon to do a bit of tidying up in the parlor. You eat a decent dinner and try to get some rest tonight."

Jessie assured her that she would, then took a step back and waved until the car was out of sight.

She went inside and found the Ratcliffs sitting together on the sofa in the parlor. They were conversing quietly and finishing a last cup of coffee. Both of them automatically rose to their feet when she entered the room.

"It's time we were going, too, Jessie," said Dorothy Ratcliff. "You've had people in and out of this house for days. I imagine you would like a little peace and quiet."

"It has been hectic."

Richard spoke up. "I didn't see Mitch leave."

She felt a sudden chill and wrapped her arms around herself. "He's still out back somewhere...."

The professor slowly shook his head from side to side. "He's taking it hard, Jessie."

In a quiet voice she said, "I know."

His wife made a perceptive observation. "I'm not sure anyone has ever loved Mitch quite like Christine did."

Richard Ratcliff set his coffee cup down on the table with a shaky hand. "She had a special gift that way. She seemed to sense who needed her most."

Jessie tried to swallow the lump in her throat. "I'll look after Mitch now."

This announcement was met with a poignant moment of silence.

Dorothy dropped a kiss on her cheek and said, "I'll call on Wednesday and we'll get started on the acknowledgments."

"I don't know how I can ever thank you." She choked. "You've both been wonderful."

The professor gave her a paternal buss and murmured: "You're a very special young woman, Jessie. You're more like her than you know."

After the Ratcliffs had gone, Jessie found herself alone in the big old farmhouse for the first time. Evening gradually descended. She went from room to room, switching on a lamp here, drawing a shade there, as had been her grandmother's custom.

It was deathly quiet.

She slipped a sweater around her shoulders and went in search of Mitch.

Following the distinctive ring of an ax hitting its mark, Jessie found him behind the barn splitting logs into kindling and firewood.

He had removed his suit jacket and tossed it over the seat of a small John Deere tractor. His shirt sleeves were rolled up to the elbows. Beads of perspiration had formed on his brow, and his shirt was matted to his underarms and back.

She could see the sheer strength in the muscles of his arms and shoulders as he moved with the natural rhythm of the task. It was hard physical labor, and he had obviously been at it for some time.

Every now and then he bent over and wiped his face on his shirtsleeve. His skin was damp with perspiration. Or was it tears?

There were bits of wood in his hair and on his face. Small clean fragrant chips clung to his damp clothing, trouser legs, shoes, even his eyelashes.

Jessie circled him, giving the broad swing of the ax a wide berth, so Mitch would see her first from the front and not be startled.

The ax hesitated at the top of his swing, then came down with a resounding *crack*, and the log split neatly in two. It was another five minutes before he stopped and stooped over to pile up the firewood.

"There must be enough here for all of next winter," Jessie speculated.

"It was a job that needed to be done sooner or later." He glanced up and saw the expression on her face. "I guess *I* needed to do it now."

He didn't have to explain. This time she understood. He needed the physical outlet.

She saw none of the anger, none of the hatred on his face as she had that day in his basement. Whatever demons he had been trying to exorcise on that other afternoon had apparently been put at rest, if only temporarily. Today there was simply a kind of sadness in his eyes.

She crossed her arms in front of her and leaned back against the side of the barn. "Where did you learn to split wood like a pro?"

"I used to do odd jobs for people."

She was curious. There was still so much about him that she didn't know. "Before you went into the navy?"

"Yeah, before the navy."

"But after you ran away from home?"

His features were impassive, and he seemed disinclined to discuss the subject. "It was after I left home."

What had those years been like for him between leaving home at sixteen and joining the navy at eighteen, she wondered. Had Mitch been forced to chop wood in exchange for a place to sleep, or even a plate of food to eat? Had he often gone hungry? Had he been homeless? Cold and wet and alone?

Esther's words came back to her: *"I seen it in his eyes once. Mark my words, that one has been hurt and hurt bad."*

Jessie studied him now. She could see the hurt on his face. He was hurting, and hurting bad.

The wise old housekeeper had also said to her that day that Mitch needed a little mothering, a little kindness. Mothering might be something she'd had no practice at. But she could be kind. It was the least she could do.

"You look hot and tired. How about coming inside for a cold drink?"

"I'd love to." He picked up his suit jacket, hooked it with his thumb and threw it casually over his shoulder. "I should clean up first."

"There's soap, fresh towels, everything you need in the bathroom off the kitchen," she said as they strolled toward the farmhouse.

The screen door squeaked noisily as Mitch opened it for her. "I'll try to fix that for you tomorrow," he said. "Probably just needs a little oil on the hinges."

She tossed over her shoulder, "You are handy."

"You have no idea," he said with a meaningful inclination of his head.

"Hungry?"

"God, no." He patted his flat belly. "All I did this afternoon was eat." Remembering his manners, he said to her, "Thank you, anyway."

"How about a cold beer after you wash up?"

"That sounds great," he said, heading for the bathroom.

After a moment Jessie could hear the water running in the basin. She opened the door of the refrigerator and took out a can of beer. She set it on the table, then went through the motions of pouring herself a glass of lemonade.

Mitch reemerged a few minutes later. He had managed to get rid of most of the sweat and the wood chips. His hair was damp at the nape and he'd obviously run a comb through it.

"Thanks." He flipped the tab on the can and took a long swallow of beer.

"You're welcome."

She took a sip of her lemonade, and watched as his Adam's apple bobbed up and down as he drank. He let out a long, contented sigh and wiped his mouth with the back of his hand. He leaned back against the counter and crossed one foot over the other. "Everybody else gone?"

"Yes." She looked around the deserted kitchen. "The house seems so empty somehow."

He studied her for a moment or two. "Have you ever stayed out here in the country by yourself?"

Her head came around. "No."

"You're not worried or afraid of being a woman on her own?"

She tilted her head. "I lived on my own for years in New York City. I'm not afraid to stay out here in the country by myself."

He took another swallow of cold beer. "Doesn't matter."

"Why not?"

"You're still not staying here alone."

"I'm not?"

"Nope."

She knew what was coming next.

Mitch finished off his drink, crushed the aluminum can with his bare hand and tossed it in the garbage. He looked right at her. "You've got yourself a house-guest, Jessie. I'm sleeping here tonight."

Chapter Eleven

Home in Your Arms

Was she dreaming?

Jessie found herself standing in the doorway of a rustic log cabin. Beneath her feet the wooden floor was primitive and roughly hewn. Her long skirt kept snagging on one of the boards. The air inside the enclosed space smelled of sawdust and smoke, dried herbs and whatever was boiling in the cooking pot over the open fire.

There was a rocking chair in front of the hearth and a basket of needlework beside it. The rest of the furniture in the room was a dichotomy of styles and periods: a plain workbench between a pair of exquisite eighteenth-century Philadelphia pier tables, a homemade chair of willow wood sitting alongside a beautiful mahogany highboy, and an elegant silver tea service sharing the same tabletop with a scooped-out gourd bowl.

There were wooden shutters at the windows—only two narrow openings, besides the door, and both faced the front of the log cabin. A framed portrait of a young woman hung on the chinked wall. A grandfather clock was sounding the quarter hour; there was something familiar about its distinctive chime.

Then Jessie heard a groan nearby. It came from the small bedroom in the back of the cabin. A man called out in a delirious fit. His words were slurred and failed to make any sense to her. "Get thee away! I say, get thee away!"

She knew she should go to him, tend to him, wipe his fevered brow. She started toward the lean-to when the thundering of horses' hooves in the farmyard stopped her dead in her tracks and brought her head sharply around.

There were three—no, four—of them: strangers dressed in buckskin breeches and shirts, jugs in one hand, muskets in the other. They were whooping like drunkards and calling each other by name.

Before she could shut and bolt the cabin door, they spotted her.

"Hey, Dingus, lookee here, would ye? We done found ourselves a purty little lady to entertain us'n."

One of his companions made a crude remark that brought the color flooding to her cheeks. For the first time since the men had ridden into the homestead she was truly afraid. Her heart was pounding in her breast. She wanted to open her mouth and scream, but she had no voice.

She knew there was no help to be had from the man inside the cabin. He was burning up with the Fever. He hadn't recognized her in days.

She clutched a handwoven shawl around her, as if it could somehow afford her protection as well as warmth. She frantically searched the horizon, hoping to see someone, anyone, knowing full well that their nearest neighbor was miles away.

"I got an empty belly needs fillin'," complained a man the others had called Maggot. "Mayhap there's some victuals inside. Somethin' smells mighty good."

One of the marauders threw his corn liquor jug to the ground and swung off his mount: a yellowish dun-colored animal with a black mane and a black tail to match. "Got me a terrible itch that needs scratchin'," he announced with a lecherous smirk as he swaggered toward the cabin door.

Jessie tried to move her arms and legs, and discovered that she had no control over her body. She seemed frozen to the spot. Even if she could manage to make a break for it, she would never reach the rifle in time: it was propped up against the far wall of the cabin.

Besides, there were four of them and only one of her.

She closed her eyes for a moment and whispered a quick, fervent prayer.

A hand clamped over her mouth. There was heavy breathing in her ear. Sharp teeth sunk into the tender flesh of her throat. Cruel hands tore at her clothing. She wanted to retch. The stench of sour spirits on the man's breath was sickening, the stink of sweat and urine and unwashed male body overwhelming. There was an awful laugh as he clawed at her; her hair came tumbling down around her shoulders.

Despite the teachings that had been gently drummed into her since birth, she hit at her assailant with her fists, harder and harder, again and again.

May the Good Lord forgive her for meeting violence with violence, she silently intoned.

"Fightin' like a she-cat, ain't she?" snickered one of the other marauders.

She opened her eyes and saw a stream of red spittle trickling from the side of the ugly, leering mouth poised above her. She was both horrified and glad at what she had done. She wished she was bigger and stronger.

The man brought his hand back and struck her across the face. The blow sent her reeling. He hit her so hard that the teeth rattled in her head, her knees buckled beneath her, and she felt sick to her stomach again. It was then she knew for certain she would lose this battle of brute strength.

She did not give up.

She did not give in.

But she could hear the other men hooting and whistling and calling out encouragement to their companion. She tentatively raised a hand to her face and it came away spotted with blood—her blood.

The man came at her a second time. He grabbed her by the arm and viciously jerked her to her feet. She swayed against him and was repulsed to find herself in such close proximity to the monster. She wanted to run away but knew that her legs would refuse to carry her.

He tried to put his mouth on hers and she quickly turned her face away. His lips found only the cheek already turning black-and-blue from the blow he had dealt her. He swore under his breath and called her names, horrible names. He told her all the things he was going to do to her, and she nearly fell to the ground in a faint.

One thought only clamored loudly in her brain. One terrified cry for help passed her lips. *"Where are thee, Nathaniel? Dear God in heaven, where are thee?"*

"WHERE ARE THEE, Nathaniel? Dear God in heaven, where are thee?" came the piercing cry in the night.

Mitchell Jade shot straight up in bed. Something had brought him out of a deep sleep.

His blood ran cold.

A woman had screamed.

Jessie had screamed!

He tossed the sheet aside in the same instant his bare feet hit the floor. He was across the room and out the door before the sound of her voice had died away.

There was no light on in the upstairs hallway, yet he knew exactly which room was hers. He turned the doorknob and burst into Jessie's bedroom.

Moonbeams permeated the darkness, revealing the figure in the old-fashioned four-poster. Her arms were wildly flailing the air, as if she were fighting off some unseen assailant. Her short nightgown was bunched up around her waist, and her hair hung in tangles around her shoulders. Tears streamed down her face in tiny rivulets. Her eyes were wide open, but Mitch doubted that she saw anything but the horror that existed in her mind.

She was having a nightmare.

In three giant steps he was by her side. He sat down on the edge of the bed and began to gently croon to her: "Jessie. Wake up, Jessie. You're having a bad dream. It's only a bad dream, sweetheart."

She struck out at him; the blow missed its mark. "No—!"

She was trembling from head to toe; he could hear her teeth chattering. He reached out and tentatively touched her. The night was warm, but her skin was ice-cold.

He began the litany again. "It's nothing but a bad dream, Jessie. That's all. It's not real. It's time to wake up."

More than his words, Mitch was convinced later, it was the sound of his voice that finally penetrated the terror that held her in its grip.

Her arms gradually stopped their uncontrolled movements and fell limply to her sides. Her sobs became intermittent, then ceased altogether. She finally blinked several times and closed her eyes.

The next time she opened them she looked straight into his and burst into tears, blubbering: "M-Mitch—"

He opened his arms, and, wordlessly, she flew into them, knocking him off balance.

He held her close to him. He smoothed her hair back from her wet face and repeated in a singsong voice: "It's all right, babe. I'm here. I'll take care of you. There's nothing to be afraid of now."

How long he went on holding her and reassuring her, Mitchell Jade never knew. It could have been minutes, it could have been hours. He lost all track of time. But there came a point eventually when he realized Jessie was nearly herself again.

She sat back against the pillows and heaved a gigantic sigh. "I was having a nightmare."

"I guessed as much."

There was a box of tissues on the bedside table. He plucked one out and handed it to her.

She dabbed at her face. "I'm sorry I woke you up."

"There's no need to apologize."

"It was my screams, wasn't it?" she murmured, shredding the damp tissue in her hands. "I do remember screaming."

God, he wanted to take her into his arms again and love her, cherish her, hold her close to him and never let her go! He tried to assure her. "It doesn't matter, Jessie girl. Believe me, it's not the first time I've awakened to the sound of screams."

She wadded the tissue into a small ball and dropped it into the wastepaper basket by the bed. "*Whose* screams woke you up?"

He knew what she was asking. He wouldn't lie to her. "My own."

Her chin came up, trembling. "Oh, Mitch—"

As gently as he could, he told her: "We all have our nightmares, Jessie."

She leaned forward and put her head down on his shoulder. "I know." Another great sigh. "I'd rather not be alone right now. Do you mind staying a little longer?"

"I don't mind. In fact, I'd like to stay."

By unspoken mutual consent they stretched out side by side on the bed. Jessie tugged at her nightgown, apparently aware it was twisted around her torso. Even more aware, perhaps, that he was lying beside her in the middle of the night, wearing only a pair of scant jockey shorts.

The minutes slipped by. Her breathing became normal, but Mitch sensed on some gut-level that she wasn't asleep.

He turned his head on the down-filled pillow and stared at her profile etched against the night. "Do you want to talk about it?"

She shrugged, uncertain.

Somehow the darkness made it easier to talk. At least that had been his experience. He remembered the long nights aboard ship when the sailors had lain in their bunks, smoking a last cigarette and speaking of home, of wives and girlfriends, of fears and dreams, life and

death. No wonder he'd come to regard the navy as
home, his buddies as family.

The night could be Jessie's friend, as well. If she
would let it. The comfort of knowing she was cloaked
in shadows that hid her from prying eyes, that con-
cealed unsightly bruises—mental as well as physical.
Yes, the night, the darkness, could be a good friend,
indeed.

A disembodied voice he scarcely recognized as Jessie's said finally: "It was awful. Worse than awful. It
was frightening." The woman beside him on the bed
shivered violently. "It was—terrifying."

Mitch held his breath and kept silent. He wasn't
about to claim that he knew what she had gone through.
Maybe he did. Then again, maybe he didn't.

She vigorously rubbed the flesh on her arms as if to
ward off a sudden chill. "Strangers, marauders, rode
into our homestead. There were four of them. They
were armed and they'd been drinking." In a voice
sharpened by fear she said, "One of the men attacked
me."

"Oh my God, Jessie."

A hoarse whisper was directed toward him. "I called
out for Nathaniel, for you, didn't I?"

He sucked in his breath. "Yes."

"What did I say?"

He had to be careful. "You don't remember?"

"Only a vague recollection."

Mitch turned onto his side and propped his head up
on one hand. With the other hand, he reached out and
brushed a strand of hair back from her face. He stroked
her, soothed her. It was some time before he answered
her question. "You were afraid and you cried out:

'Where are thee, Nathaniel? Dear God in heaven, where are thee?' "

Even in the darkness he could see the tears that formed in her eyes and slowly slid down her face. He moved closer and pressed his mouth to her cheek, tasting the salt on the tip of his tongue, wishing there was something he could do to take away the pain.

"Don't cry, Jessie." It tore him apart to see her cry. "It was only a dream."

"Do you think so?"

God, he hoped so. "I know so." He had to keep talking. "I'm here now. You'll be all right. I promise."

One minute followed another and still her tears did not stop. Then he sensed that something had changed.

He drew her into his arms. "What is it, honey?"

A muffled, "It hurts."

"What hurts?"

"Knowing that I'll never see her again."

He didn't have to ask. He knew. She was talking about her grandmother, her dearest Grandmama, his own Christine.

It broke his heart.

Despite his attempt to offer her consolation, Mitch's voice was heavy with sorrow. "You said it yourself. She's with your grandfather now and there's no place in heaven or on earth that she would rather be."

Empty words. Shallow words. Meaningless words. Not words of solace. There was no solace to be found in the death of her grandmother and his friend.

Mitch bit back his own tears. It hurt like hell, and nothing was going to change that.

"You miss her, too, don't you?"

He nodded. "Sometimes I still can't believe she's gone," he said into the blackness of the night.

"Neither can I."

Their eyes met in the darkness. "I did love her, Jessie."

A whispered, "I know. And she loved you."

"She was all gentleness and goodness." He held her gaze with his own. "You're very much like her."

"I would like to be."

Silence.

He pulled her to him and touched her mouth with his: once, twice, three times. A kiss meant to console. A kiss meant to say he cared. A kiss that was gentle and kind and comforting. Because that was what she needed from him.

His heart was full. The words came to his lips and he whispered them into the night: "I love you, Jessie."

"And I love you, Mitch."

She curled up in the warmth of his arms, and, with their bodies entwined, they fell asleep.

DAWN WAS APPROACHING on the eastern horizon when Jessie awoke. It was that suspended moment of time between day and night, night and day. The sky was gray velvet, the world still, the birds silent. All of that would soon change. Daybreak and dusk: they were both brief.

It took Jessie no more than a second or two to realize someone was beside her in bed. She had slept alone for too many years *not* to know.

It was Mitch.

He was sound asleep. Lying on his back, one arm was tucked behind his head, the other was flung out over the edge of the mattress. The covers had been kicked aside sometime in the night, but he seemed unperturbed, untroubled. It provided her the perfect opportunity to study him.

The blue-black pelt covering his head was a bit mussed; he appeared all the more attractive for it. The patches of hair under his arms were lighter in color and had a soft, baby-fine texture to them. There was a smattering on his chest that arrowed down his torso and abdomen, and disappeared into the waistband of his shorts. He had enough body hair to be thoroughly masculine, without going to extremes.

Mitchell Jade was obviously in superb physical condition for a man in his mid-thirties. He was lean and muscular and there was not a spare ounce of flesh on the magnificent body.

And there was very little of his body she couldn't see for herself.

Watching him created the oddest feeling in the pit of her stomach. She wasn't completely naive, yet she was scarcely a woman of the world, either. Any intelligent man or woman had to be fastidious in this day and age. It was the only wise way to conduct one's life.

Her eyes scanned his toes, moved up his ankles and legs to the muscular thighs, higher over the taut belly, then the muscular chest to the broad shoulders and finally to the face.

It was a face of contrasts: a hard jawline and soft lips, a broken nose and perfectly shaped ears, beautiful eyes and two emphatic slashes of dark determined brow.

Her attention focused at last on the white jagged scar on his chin, the one he'd claimed had been the result of a childhood accident. He hadn't told her everything, she was positive about that. Jessie wondered what the real story was.

She reached out and, with the tip of her index finger, gently traced the outline of the scar. She went up on her elbows. She leaned over the sleeping form and carefully lowered her mouth to his chin. She kissed him.

"Kiss it and make it better," came the murmured entreaty.

His eyes slowly opened. They were a color Jessie had never seen before: vivid green, vibrant green.

So alive.

Afire, like a rare and precious emerald.

She held her breath.

He didn't move.

Once again she asked the question. "How did you get the scar on your chin?"

She could feel the heavy thud, thud, thud of his heart beating beneath her fingertips, fingertips that rested lightly on his bare chest as she bent over him.

"Do you really want to know?"

There was no pretense in her reply. "I want to know everything there is to know about it."

"The whole truth?"

"The whole truth and nothing but the truth."

His eyes blazed. "Even if it isn't pretty?"

"*Especially* if it isn't pretty."

He sighed. "It's all in the past."

With a full heart, Jessie believed every word she said to him. "Nothing is ever 'all in the past.' Whatever we *were* has made us whatever we *are*."

His voice was low and husky as he reached up and tucked an errant strand of hair behind her ear. "Sometimes you're wise beyond your years."

"I'm not a child, Mitch," came the gentle reminder. "I'm a woman and I'll soon be thirty years old."

After a moment, he said: "I'm thirty-six and I can't ever remember being young."

She wanted to cry. Instead, she kissed his chin again and prompted: "The scar?"

"I don't know where to begin," he confessed.

A bittersweet smile tugged at her mouth as she uttered the obvious comeback. "At the beginning?"

"I don't know the beginning."

She stretched out beside him; their bodies only a fraction of an inch apart, but not touching. "Then start with the year you were nine."

His eyes darkened. "The year I was nine..."

Jessie almost stopped him right there and then, suddenly afraid, suddenly knowing that what he was about to tell her was going to be painful for both of them. But she held on and she held her tongue.

He started to explain. "In some families there is one kid, it seems, singled out to take the brunt of whatever the parents are dishing out. Psychologists and other professionals are only now beginning to understand this type of child abuse."

Jessie shivered from head to toe.

Mitch went on. "The parents seem to pick one kid to vent their anger and frustration and abuse on. There have even been documented cases of one kid being starved while the others in the family are fed, beaten while other children are lavished with affection, locked away in a closet while everyone else is treated normally." He turned his head on the pillow and looked at her, watching for signs that she was recoiling from the awful truth of what he was relating.

Jessie steeled herself for what was to come. She was determined to be brave, to hear what she was sure this man had never told another human being. She was not going to be fainthearted.

She was not going to give up.

She was not going to give in.

Whatever unspeakable, horrible things had happened to him, she wanted Mitch to know that he could tell her, that he could share the worst of his life with her and she would not back away, she would not love him any less.

Indeed, she would love him all the more.

"Anyway, maybe it was because I was the oldest of the five children my parents had. Maybe it was some natural animosity between my personality and theirs. Maybe it was because I never bothered to hide my disdain for their drinking and their screaming and their way of life—" he shrugged and gave the pillow behind his head an absentminded punch or two "—but from the time I was about six or seven, possibly even younger, I became the object of my mother and father's abuse."

Jessie reached out and carefully enfolded his larger hand in her smaller one.

"At least it seemed to save my younger brother and sisters. They were too little to understand."

"You were too little to understand, too," she blurted out in his defense.

"Somehow I did understand, Jessie, and I started to live on the streets as much as I could, only coming home at night to sleep. Sometimes not even then. Especially if my parents were on a binge. It was ten times worse when they'd been drinking. That's how I got this scar."

"They hit you?"

His mouth formed a crooked line. "One night I forgot to duck, and ended up hitting my chin on the coffee table in the living room. A couple of neighbors rushed me to the emergency room. They claimed it took ten stitches to close the cut." He shrugged his shoul-

ders as if to say he hadn't bothered to count them. "I
never shed a tear. Not one."

For perhaps the second time in her life, Jessie was
filled with a sense of uselessness, of utter futility. She
had not been there to save her parents. She had not been
there to save Mitch. With all her heart and soul she
wished she could have been. . . .

"As I got older and bigger, the abuse became verbal,
instead of physical. Everyone seemed to blame me for
whatever troubles came along, conveniently forgetting
that it had begun long before I could be held responsible. The younger kids didn't seem in any danger. As a
matter of fact, I began to wonder if it was my fault, too,
because the whole family seemed to be better off if I
wasn't around. So the day I turned sixteen, I packed up
my few belongings and walked out the door, vowing
never to return."

"What about your mother's funeral?"

"A friend let me know about that. I stood in the back
of the church and my brother and sisters and my father
filed past me without saying a word. I haven't spoken
to them and they haven't spoken to me in twenty years.
I told you they were better off without me."

She wanted to bawl. "You know none of it was your
fault."

"Intellectually I do, but that doesn't mean that I
don't carry the same genes, the same awful possibilities
around in my own body."

"You are not the bad seed, Mitchell Jade." Tears
welled up at the edge of Jessie's eyelids. Tears of sorrow. Tears of rage. "You were a little boy abused in the
worst way by a sick, cruel family."

There was absolute conviction in his voice when he
told her, "I have no family."

After a pause, she inhaled deeply and whispered to him in the night: "I understand now. Those people are not your family, they never were. But others can become your family—good friends, those who love you."

She knew his heart was laid bare when he admitted: "Your grandmother was as close as I've ever gotten to knowing what it would be like to have a mother."

Jessie opened herself to him. "In many ways, Grandmama was more a mother to me than my own mother."

"We're both orphaned now."

"Yes, we are, aren't we?" She searched his eyes. "Perhaps we can create something together."

"I don't know, Jessie. I don't know if I have it in me to do that."

There was so much at stake. "You'll never know if you don't give it a chance, if you don't try."

"That's what Christine made me promise once."

"What did Grandmama make you promise?"

"To give us a chance. I had just told her that I wasn't any good for a woman like you."

"I'd like to be the judge of that, but you haven't given me an opportunity to find out." She knew there was a funny little smile on her face. "Maybe we should start at the beginning and see what happens."

He turned onto his side again and faced her squarely. "And just what is the beginning?"

She was suddenly aware of his size, his strength, his near nudity. "We could begin with a kiss."

"We've kissed before," he pointed out.

"For the sake of argument, let's say we haven't."

Mitch's expression was one of skepticism. "I'm supposed to kiss you?"

"Something like that."

His mouth unfolded into a lazy grin. "Something like that?"

"Exactly like that, then."

He seemed to be double-checking. "For the sake of our mutual experiment."

"For our mutual sake."

His voice sent little whispers down her spine. "Come here."

"I am here."

"Closer."

Her pulse was racing. She moved closer. The temptation to kiss him was quickly becoming a matter of life and death. Still, she managed to hold back several inches from his mouth.

He reached up and clasped the back of her neck with his hand and brought her face down to within a fraction of an inch of his. "I sure as hell hope you know what you're asking for."

So did she.

Then he crushed his mouth to hers in a kiss that exploded on impact. It sent her reeling. It took all of her previous experience with kisses and blanked them out as if they had never existed. Indeed, they never had. He made her hunger and thirst for him. He gave her everything, and left her wanting more. He took, yet somehow she received.

"Give me your sweet mouth," he whispered fiercely.

Jessie obeyed. Then he slipped between her half-open lips and was inside her: tasting, sucking, licking, teasing, giving, taking, tempting, asking, demanding, begging—all with his lips and his teeth and his tongue. She had never known that so much could be done with so little.

She had never realized the lengths to which passion could drive a man and a woman. Her head was spinning. Her heart was pounding. Her mind was dumbfounded and confounded. She was now a creature of emotions, not reason. She was a woman of sensuality, not intellect. She was physical, not mental.

She was all feelings and sensations, needs and desires. She did not recognize herself, and yet she was more herself than she had ever been in her entire life.

In a seemingly single movement her nightgown was gone and his shorts ended up in a small heap on the floor. Then he began to touch her with his great gentle hands. He caught her breasts in his palms and her nipples hardened against his callused skin. His caress created a strange ache in her, deep inside her, that was stronger than anything Jessie had ever known.

He placed his lips on her left breast and suckled, drawing her farther and farther into his mouth. Then he raised his head and claimed with elemental male satisfaction, "Your heart is pounding."

She pressed her hand to the spot above his own heart. "So is yours."

She wanted to feel his hands, his lips, his teeth on her: on her breasts, the smooth skin of her abdomen, the silky flesh on the inside of her thighs, and, between her legs, that most sensitive part of a woman's body.

His tongue parted her lips and slipped between them for an intimate kiss. In the same instant he eased a finger past her wild damp curls and into the very heart of her. She throbbed against his hand.

"Mitch—"

"It's all right, love. You must know that I want you." His eyes were suddenly burning like green fire. "I need to know that you want me."

"I do," she declared in return. "I want all of you."

He made her a promise: she would have all of him—soon.

But first she slid down his body because she wanted to know him as well as a woman can know a man. Her fragrance drifted along his flesh as she did, smoothly, lightly, enticingly. It drove him crazy. It nearly drove him over the edge.

It was his turn to call out her name in a groan of need and desire. "Jessie—"

"I'm here, Mitch," she assured him.

"I know. I know," he chanted, his fingers clutching unknowingly at the bedsheets, his breath harshly indrawn, his breathing labored, as she stroked him.

There would be no secrets between them, they had vowed. They had promised there would be only truth. There was no room for anything but the truth between a man and woman who stripped their souls bare along with their bodies. It was the ultimate act of intimacy. Making love was the ultimate act of intimacy if done with open hands and open hearts and open souls as these two were.

"Come to me," Mitch said, and she did.

"Give all of yourself to me," Jessie pleaded, and he willingly complied.

He hovered above her for a moment, then moved against her, surged into her, letting her slowly and surely take all of him.

It was sex and it was love. It was physical and it was spiritual. It was both an ending and a beginning. It was all-consuming and it was utter consummation.

And, in the aftermath of their lovemaking, they lay together, sated, satisfied. For a time, lost in the beautiful dawn and one another, they had found a home in each other's arms.

Chapter Twelve

Turning Toward Home

Mitch stood with one hand on the open refrigerator door; the other he rubbed absentmindedly back and forth across his bare chest.

He had just stepped out of the shower. His hair was damp and he hadn't bothered to shave yet, a fact attested to by the black stubble he still sported along his jaw and upper lip. He was wearing a pair of faded blue jeans. That was all.

The linoleum tile was cool beneath his feet. He took a jug of fresh orange juice from the top shelf of the refrigerator and poured himself a large glass. Then he stood at the kitchen sink and gazed out the window at the farmyard and beyond to the vast expanse of cultivated fields.

He opened the back door. There was a breeze on this fine July morning, but by midday the temperature and the humidity would both climb into the eighties.

Morning sunlight glistened on the dewy grass in the high meadow; fields of corn swayed in the summer breeze like an endless sea of lush green. There was a wind chime dangling from the overhang on the back porch. Through the open door, he could hear the sound of its tinkling glass caught up in the wind, bumping into each other again and again.

The wind through the trees, the fields of swaying corn—"knee-high by the Fourth of July"—the creaking of a barn door, the distant barking of a dog, the song of the wind chimes, the quiet, familiar movements of the woman in the bedroom overhead: these were the sounds that made up his morning.

Mitch drained the glass of icy cold orange juice, then turned his face to the east, to the rising sun, and basked for a moment in its welcome warmth, considering how good life could be. How good life was.

Too good.

He had never thought of himself as a fatalist before, but happiness was transitory—indeed, often fragile. Like a helium-inflated balloon, it didn't take much to burst its bubble. No one knew that better than he did.

Yet in many ways he had never been happier than during the few short weeks since he and Jessie had become lovers. For the first time in his life he loved and was loved in return.

Christine had been right.

"I get a special feeling when I come here," he remembered confiding to her early in the spring, after he'd been visiting the Brick farm on a weekly basis for some months. "There's something about this place...." He hadn't known how to describe it at the time.

He recalled how she had slipped her small slender hand into his and told him: "I've always felt the same way, Mitch. It's the reason I moved back here after my dear James died."

"What do you think it is?" He had wanted to know; he had needed to know.

"Perhaps something as simple as love. This house has always been filled with love," she had said to him then.

Christine had been right all along, of course, Mitch acknowledged as he went through the motions of measuring so much coffee and so much water, then flipped the switch on the automatic percolator. This was a house filled with love.

Still, darker thoughts had a tendency to steal in when he least expected them.

I'm no good for Jessie.

I don't deserve a woman of her gentleness, her intelligence, her goodness.

I will only bring her grief.

Before it's all said and done, I will make her life a living hell.

It's too late for me. I can't settle down and live the quiet life of a college professor, for God's sake.

He was trying his damnedest to take each day as it came, to not think too much about the decision that he would soon have to face. Very soon. But it was always there in the back of his mind, in the back of Jessie's mind, too, he was sure.

He loved Jessie, but that by itself wasn't necessarily enough. Not every man and woman who fell in love were any good for each other, or for the people around them. Proof in point: his own parents had supposedly loved each other. Their marriage and his childhood had been a living hell.

Time was running out. He couldn't sit on the fence forever. It wasn't fair to Jessie, or the university, or even to himself. It was time—past time, he knew—for him and Jessie to have a serious talk.

Tonight.

It had to be tonight. Tomorrow he was going to give the university his answer. Tomorrow he would commit himself to staying or going.

He frowned unhappily.

That was his lot in life: to be a harbinger of the worst it had to offer. Beware of Greeks bearing gifts. Beware of men like him, he wanted to warn Jessie.

Even on a glorious summer morning like this one, Mitch thought of all the places he had been and all the people he had seen during his years as a journalist. He had been witness to countless unspeakable acts that men had perpetrated in the name of love: love of God, love of country, love of a woman. He knew he was fully capable of all three.

He loved Jessie so he should stay. He loved Jessie so he should go. The bottom line: He was the villain either way.

"Dammit!" he swore under his breath.

Years ago he'd resigned himself to not being with anybody for the rest of his life. He had given himself a hundred good reasons why marriage wouldn't work for him. He'd said to himself: "I'm not a romantic. I don't believe in love everlasting. I'm lousy husband material, so I'll focus on my career, and that'll be my life."

Then Jessie had come along and everything changed. He loved loving her, and sometimes he hated loving her. She made him want to stay and she made him want to run away.

Still, he was here in her house now, despite his better judgment. His few stolen moments in the sun. He would bask in them while he could.

He rinsed out his juice glass and set it in the drain rack, then poured himself a mug of steaming hot coffee. He opened the refrigerator door again and took out a bottle of fresh cream: it was less than a third full. He expertly poured a little into his coffee.

Hearing Jessie's footfalls on the stairs, he called out to her: "Hey, honey, we're nearly out of fresh cream again."

"We'll stop at Popplewell's when we go out later," she said as she padded barefoot into the kitchen.

She was wearing his shirt: a soft blue chambray, sleeves rolled up past the elbows, shoulders drooping halfway down her arms, shirttails nicely covering her backside, while leaving the long, lovely length of her legs exposed.

Her hair was a glorious tangle of chestnut brown. She hadn't bothered to run a brush through it. Her face was scrubbed clean, and she smelled faintly of toothpaste and baby powder. She had an open book in her hands: it appeared to be Elizabeth Banks's diary, and, with a frown of concentration, she was simultaneously reading and chewing on her bottom lip.

Mitch could have watched her all day.

He went through the formality of inquiring: "What are you reading?"

"Hmm...Elizabeth's journal. I think I may have found something interesting."

Mitch sauntered over to her, carefully extracted the antique leather volume from her hands and placed it on the kitchen table. He drew her into the circle of his arms and leaned over to nuzzle her neck.

"I think I may have found something interesting, as well," he murmured as he pressed his lips to the pulse point just below her ear, then to a second one beating, fluttering, like the wings of a small wild bird, in the hollow of her throat.

Jessie laughed, and the sound of her laughter was unwittingly sensual and slightly husky. She wrapped her arms tightly around his waist, burying her face in the smattering of hair on his chest. She pressed her mouth to his skin and inhaled as though she loved the very essence of him. It gave him a small thrill; it always did. Then she went up on her tiptoes and dropped a quick kiss on his chin.

Before she could escape him, Mitch caught her face between his hands and kissed her. Not once. Not twice. But again and again, until they were both out of breath and nearly giddy with the joy they took in each other.

He should leave her alone, but he couldn't seem to get his fill of her. His appetite for her was insatiable, and he didn't mean totally on a sexual level. He simply loved being with her. He loved talking to her, listening to her, kissing her, sleeping beside her, holding her in his arms, inhaling that distinctive scent that was hers and hers alone that seemed to defy description. He knew she never wore perfume, so he couldn't figure out what made her smell so good, so wholly irresistible.

She put her head back and looked up at him. "I was reading a fascinating passage in Elizabeth's diary this morning."

Nudging the material of the chambray shirt aside with his nose and mouth, he trailed a provocative chain of kisses across her exposed shoulder, and said in a throaty rumble: "I don't want to live in the past, Jessie. I want the here and now."

He heard her breath catch, felt her pulse quicken. "I know what you want."

His body thickened. "Then you must know I want it here and now."

A woman's smile appeared on her face. "Here and now?"

He barely managed a "Yes."

She rubbed up against him, and suddenly he was the one who couldn't seem to catch his breath.

His hands went to the buttons down the front of her shirt: underneath she was naked polished ivory.

Her hands went to the zipper down the front of his jeans: he knew she would find him ready to love her.

He touched her here and here and here, and each time he felt the tiny gasp of surprise she gave, only to be followed by a sigh of pleasure. With him she blossomed into a loving, sensuous woman. It was one of the things he adored most about her—she thoroughly enjoyed their relationship on this elemental physical level.

He found her hidden sweetness. He clasped her around the hips and lifted her onto him. She fit perfectly. Then he began to move, slowly at first, then with greater urgency. It was an age-old rhythm, the rhythm of lovemaking.

"Mitch!" She cried out with his name on her lips, and clung to him with a kind of mindless rejoicing.

They went to that place where no one else could follow, where only lovers may go: a world created by the two of them, a world all their own.

Mitch felt stronger, stronger than he had ever felt before. He could be anyone, do anything, he was triumphant, invincible, he could conquer the whole world, the whole universe, if he had a mind to.

She discovered once again that the emptiness, the loneliness inside could be filled through surrender, and through her surrender she became the victor, as well.

"As I STARTED to explain before I was interrupted earlier this morning—" Jessie's cheeks grew warm with the remembrance of her own abandoned behavior in this very kitchen, and his "—I believe I've found a passage in Elizabeth's journal that explains the nightmare I had that first night."

Mitch's attention was diverted from the plate of country ham and fried eggs in front of him. He quickly swallowed the food in his mouth and said, genuinely puzzled: "You believe it explains your nightmare?"

"I think so." She took a sip of hot coffee and pushed her mug safely to one side. "If you'll bear with me, I'll begin with the entries leading up to the incident."

"I'm all ears," he assured her.

She opened the leather-bound book and read aloud to him in an excited voice:

January 3, 1822

The weather has been cold and bitter since the New Year. Tho the men did pack down eight inches of Henry County clay for the cabin floor and cover it with white sand, it is not as warm as the puncheon floor Joshua and Nathaniel have promised to put in before next month.

I have been feeling poorly and full of humours. Perhaps it is from eating heavily of corn bread and pork. I did take to my bed for three days a fortnight ago. I do hold the melancholia partly to blame.

February 2, 1822

I do believe that Nathaniel and the livestock are at advantage living in the barn. At least it is large and the cows do give off excessive heat to warm him body and soul.

February 8, 1822

The weather has been most pleasant this past week, and I am feeling the better for it. Joshua has taken the dogs and gone off hunting for fresh venison or wild duck. He cannot bear to be housed up all winter in our small cabin, this I do know. At least I have my wooden floor now.

February 14, 1822

My hand does tremble so when I try to write about the terrible thing that has occurred. Today Joshua's horse did return home without him. There was a deer and a pheasant tied across the hindquarters.

Nathaniel did take his rifle then and go in search of Joshua. He did tell me later that he found him little more than a mile from our Homestead, the dogs standing guard over his wounded body. Being an Expert in such matters from his soldiering days, Nathaniel was able to remove the bullet he found in Joshua's shoulder.

My husband has been Delirious with Fever these past four days, but we have made some sense out of his rambling talk. It does seem there was trouble among a group of drunken Marauders who had ridden into the County from parts Unknown. Joshua did try to keep the peace and was shot by one of the men in a fit of anger. This is all we know at present.

February 25, 1822

I cannot bear to think of what I have done....

It did begin three days ago. Joshua was confined to his bed and still Feverish. Nathaniel had gone to town as we must have fresh supplies, nearly being out of flour and sugar, which is very dear, and tea.

All of a sudden I did hear men riding into our clearing, whooping and hollering and carrying on in a Drunken Manner. I was sore afraid.

One of the marauders did force his way into our cabin before I could reach Joshua's rifle. He came at me. My dress was torn in the ensuing struggle, and he did strike me a most angry and ferocious blow.

Just when I had given up all hope of help, dear Nathaniel rode into the Homestead. He did come at a full gallop with his firearm in hand, and order the men to quit this place in a commanding voice I had never before heard him use.

Three of the strangers did depart, riding off at breakneck speed, but one raised his weapon and pointed it at Nathaniel. He did not see the threat. I knew what I must do. I went for my husband's rifle...

Nathaniel has assured me that I did save his life. It is of some comfort for me to believe that it is so.

February 26, 1822

May God forgive me one day for breaking His holy commandment. I cannot forgive myself.

Jessie's voice trailed off into silence.

Mitch had long since finished eating his breakfast. He sat, unmoving, a lukewarm mug of coffee suspended in midair, obviously enthralled and brimming with curiosity.

He said, "Well?"

She looked up. "Well what?"

He failed to hide his impatience. "What happened after that? What holy commandment couldn't Elizabeth forgive herself for breaking?"

She appeared nonplussed. "I don't know."

"Didn't you read any further?"

"Of course, I did."

"What does she write about it?"

"Nothing."

Mitch set his mug down on the kitchen table and gave her a skeptical look. "Nothing?"

Jessie gave a decisive nod of her head. "Not a word. I've read ahead for days, for weeks, even for months, and Elizabeth never mentions the incident again."

He sat back in his chair and stroked his chin thoughtfully. "That's odd."

"You can say that again." She took a sip from her own mug. It was quickly followed by a grimace: her coffee was both cold and bitter.

Mitch stared off into the distance and murmured: "I wonder what happened." He brought his attention back to her. "What do you think it was?"

"What do I think *what* was?"

"The broken commandment."

She speculated. "Elizabeth said that she had broken God's holy commandment. It sounds like one of the Ten Commandments to me."

"You mean like 'Thou shalt not steal'?"

She nodded, and recited the list from memory.

He was astonished.

She hurriedly explained, turning pink. "I had perfect attendance in Sunday School."

"I don't doubt it for a minute."

She nervously drummed her fingers on the tabletop. "Through the process of elimination, I believe we can narrow the list down considerably."

Mitch agreed with her. "I'll bet it was a case of adultery."

She arched her brow at him. "Back to your 'eternal triangle' theory?"

"Sounds reasonable to me."

"I don't know why, but I don't believe it was adultery. Not in the physical sense, anyway."

He shook his head, bewildered. "The whole thing is . . . strange."

"Yes, it is."

He looked right at her. "Does it resemble your nightmare?"

"As far as I can remember, it does." She made a small nervous gesture with both hands. "You were wrong about one thing, however."

"I was?"

Jessie swallowed. "It wasn't just a dream. It really did happen. Only it happened to Elizabeth Banks."

They both jumped when the shrill ring of the telephone on the kitchen wall sliced through the air.

Jessie answered on the third ring. "Hello."

"That you, Jessie girl?"

She responded with, "Good morning, Seth."

The farmer-turned-antiques-expert spoke in his customary country drawl: "You two going to be out and about later this morning?"

"As a matter of fact, we are." There was no sense in being coy about it: everybody in Henry County knew that Mitch had literally moved in with her some weeks before. But, bless their hearts, not a soul had said a disparaging word to her. "Mitch and I were about to drive over to Popplewell's to pick up a few groceries."

"Would you have time to stop by the shop afterward?" came the guarded question.

"Of course, we would." Then a little anxiously she inquired: "Is everything all right, Seth? Nothing's happened to you or Alice, has it?"

"No, no, we're both fine," he quickly reassured her. "I just want to show you something."

She immediately had an idea and brightened. "You've got Elizabeth's sampler framed, haven't you? I'll bet it looks splendid."

"That isn't it, exactly," said Seth, and Jessie could just see the dear man pulling on his beard—now as much white as it was brown—as he stood awkwardly by the desk in his office and talked into the plain black telephone the Hillocks had had as long as she could remember.

She was curious, but recognized Seth's natural reluctance to discuss the matter until she was there in person.

It was only neighborly of her to offer: "Does Alice need anything from the general store?"

His reply was vague. "Don't rightly know."

"Do you want to check with her and see?"

"Alice is in the kitchen making a pot of tea."

"A pot of tea?" Jessie repeated.

That was odd. The Hillocks were strictly coffee drinkers, always had been. Tea was for medicinal purposes only in their house.

She had to ask again. "Are you sure you're both feeling all right?"

"Fit as a fiddle, that's Alice and me." Then he lowered his usual booming baritone ever so slightly and spoke directly into the mouthpiece of the telephone: "Don't know if I can say the same about—" he cleared his throat and attempted to whisper "—Becky Sue, though."

"Becky Sue Stoots?"

"That's the one."

"Is she ill?"

"Nope."

"Is the baby okay?"

"Yup."

"Lyman?"

"Lyman's fine."

"What is it, then?"

"Can't rightly say."

"Why not?"

"Won't stop crying long enough to tell us. Blubbering like a baby. Weeping buckets. Been through half a box of tissues since she got here."

"Becky Sue?"

"That's the one."

There were times when getting information from the likes of Seth Hillock was as difficult as pulling teeth. The process took an infinite amount of patience and determination, not to mention skill.

She sighed and assured him: "We'll be over as soon as we make a quick stop at Popplewell's."

"You do that, Jessie girl."

"Goodbye, Seth."

But he'd already rung off on his end.

She hung up the receiver and slowly turned to Mitch.

He was shaking his head and chuckling softly to himself, apparently amused by what he had heard of her conversation. "You appear puzzled."

She frowned. "That's because I *am* puzzled."

"I assume that was Seth Hillock."

"You assume correctly."

He pushed his chair back, got to his feet and proceeded to carry his dirty breakfast dishes to the kitchen sink. "What did he want?"

"That's where the puzzled part comes into it."

Mitch turned on the hot water faucet, squirted a puddle of dishwashing liquid onto a sponge and began to scrub the dried egg off his plate. He held out a soapy palm and Jessie handed him the coffee mugs and the frying pan from the stove.

He prompted. "Seth wants—?"

She finally told him. "Seth wants to show me something."

"What?"

"I don't know." Anticipating Mitch's next question, she added, "He didn't say."

"In other words, we don't really know the who, what, where, when or how of it?"

"Huh?"

He elucidated: "That's basic reporter talk for finding out what the hell's going on."

Jessie firmly planted her hands on her hips. "Well, I don't *know* what the hell's going on. I'm not sure Seth does, either. He has something to show me. That's all I know. That, and the fact that his wife is making a cup of tea for a crying girl in their kitchen."

Mitch made a gesture in the air with his wet soapy hands, and exclaimed with exaggerated relief: "Ah, now we're getting somewhere."

"Becky Sue Stoots."

He seemed to be catching on to her verbal shorthand. "I take it, she's the crying girl."

A nod. "Buckets."

"But it's nothing serious."

"Not as far as Alice and Seth can tell."

He dried his hands on the dish towel and proceeded to tick off the points on his fingers. "One, she's not ill. Two, the baby is okay. Three, Lyman is fine."

"You eavesdropped."

"I couldn't help it. I was standing right here."

"Well, that's about the size of it, anyway," she confirmed.

"We're supposed to stop by the antique barn after we do our shopping at Popplewell's?"

"I said we would."

"Then we'd better get a move on."

"DID HORATIO POPPLEWELL say anything while we were grocery shopping that you found strange?"

Mitch looked at her askance as he backed his red Corvette out of the gravel parking area at the side of the general store. "Is this one of those trick questions?"

Jessie gave him a playful nudge with her elbow and couldn't quite keep from laughing. "I'm serious. Did anything strike you as odd?"

He arched both black brows meaningfully. "Lots of things about Horatio Popplewell strike me as odd. What in particular did you have in mind?"

Jessie was going to scold him and changed her mind. Instead she said: "Not about Mr. Popplewell, but what he said about Becky Sue Stoots."

Mitch shrugged. "I guess I didn't hear him."

"He told me that only this morning Becky Sue had paid her entire overdue grocery bill."

His forehead creased. "I guess I'd find it odder if she *didn't* pay an overdue grocery bill."

Jessie fell silent, thinking about it. "The thing is, I'm pretty sure that Becky Sue and Lyman simply don't have that kind of money."

Eyes straight ahead on the road, Mitch asked: "What kind of money are we talking about here?"

"This is in the strictest confidence," she warned him.

He held up two fingers. "I won't breathe a word. Scout's honor."

She gave him one of those "doubting Thomas" looks. "Were you ever a Boy Scout?"

"No," he confessed. "But I hit one once."

"Mitch!"

"Hey, we were in the sixth grade, and the kid claimed I was obstreperous."

"Why did you hit him? Undoubtedly you were obstreperous at that age."

He appeared sheepish. "I didn't know the word meant unruly back then. I thought he was calling me a dirty name."

She raised her eyes upward, indicating the need for patience.

Mitch seemed interested in getting back to the subject of the Stoots and their grocery bill. "So how much is too much in the case of the young couple?"

"Mr. Popplewell told me that they owed him between four and five hundred dollars."

His lips pursed in a low whistle.

"My sentiments exactly," she agreed. "Not excessive by some people's standards, but certainly so in the case of a struggling farmer and his wife."

"I assume Becky Sue paid in cold hard cash."

Jessie expounded unhappily. "In crisp new one-hundred dollar bills."

He whistled again.

Her mouth turned down at the corners. "Coming on top of the news that Becky Sue is sitting in Alice's kitchen crying her eyes out, and Seth has something to show me, you can understand why I'm a little upset."

Mitch reached over and patted her hand. "Take my word for it, sweetheart. Don't go looking for trouble. It'll find you soon enough."

IT DID.

Fifteen minutes later, to be precise, when they joined Seth Hillock in his office at Hillock's Antiques.

"How's Becky Sue?" inquired Jessie with an anxious glance toward the house.

"Better. Alice is still pouring medicinal tea down her." The man apparently felt an explanation was required for Mitch's benefit. "Alice always adds a drop or two of her own special concoction at times like this."

"Alcohol?" hazarded Mitch.

The former farmer's mouth dropped open. "Heavens to Betsy, no. It's extract of spiced rhubarb, cinnamon and a dash of cloves. Wouldn't give the girl alcohol—she's expecting a baby."

Duly chastised, he kept quiet while Jessie inquired, "What is it you wanted to show me, Seth?"

The big man turned around and took a box down from the shelf behind him. He set it on the oversize desk that partially served as a worktable, and without ceremony removed the lid.

"What do you see?"

Jessie leaned over and studied the box's contents. It was magnificent. The breath caught for a moment in her throat. She blinked away a nostalgic tear, and answered in hushed tones: "I see Elizabeth's sampler in a beautiful antique frame."

Seth Hillock's lips compressed. "Look again."

This time both Jessie and Mitchell Jade bent over the box.

Mitch was the first to notice the discrepancy. "This isn't Elizabeth's sampler," he announced, straightening.

"Well, give the man a prize," Seth said without a trace of humor.

Mitch looked from Jessie to the older man and back again. "It's a fake."

Chapter Thirteen

Almost Home

Jessie was dumbfounded. "How do you know it's a fake?" She still couldn't believe what she'd heard. "After all, you're not an expert in these matters."

Mitch was in total agreement. "That's true. I know nothing about fabric, or color, or dyes, or how rare a design is, or any of the other factors Seth mentioned when we first brought Elizabeth's sampler in for framing."

"But—"

He finished quietly, "But I do have eyes to see."

"And—?" she prompted.

"And the first thing I noticed is that the 's' in the word finished is wrong," he pointed out.

Jessie looked again. She read aloud the phrase at the bottom of the antique needlework: "'Elizabeth Finished This Work In The Eleventh Year Of Her Age 1812.'" Her hand flew to her mouth. "You're absolutely right. The 's' is all wrong."

"Plain, old standard 's,'" agreed Seth. "Not in the least like the one your great-great-great-grandma worked into her embroidery."

"Pretty amateurish, too, I'd say," Mitch went on, displaying the skills that had once made him a crack investigative reporter. "Seems to me if you were going to make a copy and pass it off as the genuine article, you'd be particularly careful about a distinguishing mark like that."

Seth picked up the conversation where the younger man had left off. "Unless you never expected anyone who knew about the original to see the copy."

Jessie could tell Mitch was in his element and enjoying every minute of it; his eyes were shining bright green with interest and enthusiasm.

"Of course." He snapped his fingers together. "Whoever made this one assumed that nobody who had seen the original would learn of the fake's existence."

"Well, they were wrong," said Jessie adamantly. She looked up at Seth Hillock. "There's obviously more to the story than you've told us so far. To begin with, where did you get this sampler?"

He motioned to them to each take a seat, then sat down in his desk chair and leaned back, hands folded behind his head, and began his story. He was in no hurry.

"Jessie here knows what a 'picker' is, but I doubt if a city boy like you would." Seth Hillock crooked a shaggy brow at Mitch.

"Can't say as I do," he admitted.

"In the antiques business a 'picker' is what you would call a—"

"—contact," supplied Jessie.

"Near enough. Anyway, it's someone who keeps an eye out for a particular kind of antique, or a good bargain, or a specialty item." Seth digressed for a minute. "Good example—I got one client who buys any Art Nouveau silver pieces we can find because the little woman—" one raised eyebrow from Jessie, and the older man quickly corrected himself "—because his wife collects anything from that period—late 1800's, turn-of-the-century." He muttered under his breath, "Can't stand all that curlicue stuff myself, but it sells real well to the ladies."

For Mitch's benefit, Jessie came straight to the point. "A 'picker' buys, then turns around and tries to sell his 'picks' to a dealer for a profit."

Mitch interjected: "Sounds like a middleman."

"More like an old western scout, actually—somebody who rides ahead to check out what's over the next hill, so to speak." Seth cleared his throat and tried to stick to the subject. For a man of few words, he could be downright loquacious at times. "Anyway, Alice and me, well, we got ourselves pickers all over these United States. Some from as far away as Alaska and Maine and Texas. Hell, even New Jersey."

A kernel of an idea was beginning to form in Jessie's mind. "New Jersey?"

"New Jersey?" echoed Mitch.

"Yup. Just two days ago I get a telephone call from one of my pickers on the east coast. Seems she bought a wonderful early nineteenth-century sampler in an antique mall in Hackensack. She starts to tell me about it over the telephone, and, lo and behold—" Seth stared straight at Jessie "—if the description isn't identical to the one I just finished framing for you."

There was a stunned silence.

"I don't get it," she had to confess.

"I didn't either at first," admitted the man. "But I told her to express-mail the sampler to me pronto, and she did. It arrived yesterday. I took one look, and another, and another. Then I started doing a little snoop-

ing on my own." He got up, lumbered over to the door
of his office and called out in his great, booming voice:
"Hey, Virgil, appreciate it if you could spare us a minute."

"Sure thing, Mr. Hillock," came the answer from the
other side of the converted barn.

Moments later, Virgil Marquart—face burned by the
summer sun to a bright carrot red that matched his
hair—appeared in the doorway.

"You remember meeting Miss Jessamyn Jordan and
the professor, don't you?" prompted his employer.

"Yes, sir, I do." Virgil stuck out his hand politely and
gave first, Jessie, then Mitch, a firm handshake. "It's
nice to see you both again." He looked right at Jessie
with a confidence he hadn't possessed several months
ago. "I was really sorry to hear about your grandmother."

She managed, "Thank you, Virgil."

Seth laid a gentle hand on the teenager's shoulder.
"Now, Virgil, I'd like you to tell these folks the same
thing you told me when you came into work this morning."

"All right, Mr. Hillock." He cleared his throat and
began. "Becky Sue and I went to the same high school
out in the country. We even knew a lot of the same kids,
except she was a year ahead of me."

Seth stepped in and suggested, "I think we can skip
over that part, and go right to what happened the day
you found her in our house."

Jessie's ears pricked up. "You found Becky Sue
Stoots in the Hillocks' house?"

Virgil Marquart nodded. "I didn't think too much of
it at the time. I mean, Becky Sue used to work here and

all, and she wasn't doing anything wrong. Just looking at this old piece of cloth with some sewing on it.''

Her breath caught. ''Elizabeth's sampler.''

''It would seem so,'' said Seth.

Mitch interjected: ''Do you recall when this was, Virgil?''

The youth thought about it for a minute or two before he answered. ''I don't remember the exact date.''

''An approximate one will do,'' the former reporter said as if the answer wasn't all that urgent. He was obviously trying not to make the teenager nervous.

''I know it was before school was out for the summer 'cause I was only working for the Hillocks part-time. It could have been the first or second week of May.''

Mitch stood up and began to pace back and forth in the small office. ''It fits.''

''I dropped off the sampler at the beginning of May,'' Jessie confirmed.

Seth sat back down in the chair behind the desk. ''You go ahead with your story, boy.''

Virgil did as he was told. ''I asked Becky Sue what she was doing. She kinda jumped when she heard my voice, then laughed when she realized it was only me. She said she was fascinated by old sewing and antique needlework, stuff that wouldn't interest a man.''

''Anything else?'' questioned Mitch.

''Only that I could see she'd made a pretty detailed sketch of the design on the back of a brown paper grocery bag. Becky Sue always was good in home ec and art at school. She even won a few drawing contests.''

''How very interesting,'' murmured Mitch.

''Anyway, right after that Becky Sue folded up the paper sack, stuck it in her handbag and left without another word to me. I guess I forgot all about it until this morning."

"Understandable," someone commented.

The teenager shifted his weight from one foot to the other. "I'd like to get that shipment of 1930's farm implements from Nebraska unloaded and ready for pricing before noon. Do you need me for anything else, Mr. Hillock?"

"Nope. You've been a big help to us, Virgil. Thanks."

"Yes, thank you, Virgil," added Jessie.

"You're welcome, Miss Jordan. Anytime." He looked from Jessie to Mitch and back to Jessie. "It was nice seeing you both again."

"What a polite young man," she observed once Virgil Marquart had left the office.

Seth grunted his assent. "Hard worker, too. He'll go places one day."

For a minute, perhaps longer, nothing was said.

Then Jessie spoke, directing her comments equally to the two of them: "You do realize this had to be happening about the same time my grandmother and I were encouraging the girl to put her talents to use by selling her homemade crafts in a few of the local gift shops."

"It would appear that she decided to do as you'd suggested," ventured Mitch.

Jessie dropped her head into her hands for a moment. What in the world had Becky Sue Stoots been up to?

She raised her head. "I'm sorry but I don't believe for a minute that the girl was capable of dreaming up this whole scheme on her own."

Seth rubbed his beard.

Mitch continued his pacing.

Jessie went on with her argument. "She's a clever young woman, but this kind of scam takes someone with money and connections. Where would an eighteen-year-old farmer's wife from the rural midwest get either?"

"It's a small world now, Jessie girl," chimed in the big, bearded man.

She scowled and felt forced to contradict him. "Not that small, Seth. There's something going on here that we haven't even touched upon. I just know it."

Mitch finally stopped his pacing and stated his opinion: "I have to agree with Jessie. There's something, or someone, behind this that we know nothing about. Yet."

She inhaled a deep trembling breath. "So, what do we do next?"

"What do we do next?" Mitch was the one to step in and take charge. "We go inside the house and have a friendly little chat with Becky Sue Stoots."

ALICE HILLOCK MET THEM at the door. She lowered her already soft voice, and admonished: "I don't want you badgering the girl, Seth."

Her husband—a foot taller and easily twice her weight—blustered, "Why, Alice, I wouldn't do any such thing. You know better than that."

"I hope so. It took me nearly an hour to get her calmed down." With a sympathetic sigh, the gray-haired bespectacled matron glanced over her shoulder. "Becky Sue is a sweet young thing. It's just that she's pregnant, and she's scared." She looked back at Jessie. "She keeps mumbling to herself about how disappointed Christine would be in her. How disappointed you must be in her. How she's let us all down."

Jessie's heart went out to the younger woman. "The poor thing. I feel partly to blame."

Mitch gave her a look of incredulity. "How do you figure that?"

"I'm the one who put the idea into her head to use her skills as a needlewoman to make extra money. And I'm almost certain she embroidered the fake sampler."

Alice uttered a distracted tsk-tsk and shook her head from side to side. "You're sure it's a fake?"

"Almost one-hundred percent. The chances of two identical antique samplers existing—except for one tiny discrepancy—are astronomical, as you know. The fact that they surfaced within weeks of each other is extremely suspicious. Yes, even without an expert examination, I'm sure." Jessie sighed and reiterated, "I do feel responsible for what's happened."

Mitch shook his head. "Women!"

The older man beside him seemed to agree. "You can say that again."

"Seth Hillock, you and me are going to sit down, stay quiet and stay put," commanded Alice, pointing to two chairs on the side porch. Her tone of voice told him she would brook no argument on the subject. "Jessie and Mitch will go in first and speak with the girl."

Jessie wasn't looking forward to this. She took a deep breath, opened the screen door and walked into the Hillocks' bungalow. Mitch was right behind her.

Becky Sue Stoots was sitting on a chair in the corner of the kitchen, her feet propped up on a tapestry footrest that Jessie recognized. Alice usually kept it in the front room and only brought it out for company.

The girl's blond ponytail was coming undone in the back. Her long-lashed blue eyes were bloodshot and slightly swollen; she had obviously been crying for some time. Her hands were folded across her rounded belly, and she was nervously picking at the pink polish on her fingernails.

With great gentleness, Jessie said, "Hello, Becky Sue."

Red-rimmed eyes looked up quickly, then back down again at her hands. "Hello, Miss Jordan."

"It's okay for you to call me Jessie. In fact, I'd like it if you did."

"All right, Jessie."

"You know Professor Jade, don't you?"

"Yes."

"You can call me Mitch," he suggested with equal care.

"Okay, Mitch."

Jessie began the conversation. "You've been upset about something this morning."

The heart-shaped chin trembled. "Yes."

Tact was the key; she didn't want the girl to start crying again. Indeed, the last thing she wanted was an hysterical pregnant woman on her hands. "I don't think it's good for your baby if you get upset."

"That's what Mrs. Hillock said."

"She's right."

"She is," chimed in Mitch.

"I want my baby to be healthy."

"We all want your baby to be healthy."

She sat up a little straighter in the chair. "I want to have my baby born in a hospital where the doctors and nurses will know what to do if anything goes wrong."

Jessie cautioned herself to patience. "Of course you do. Any mother would."

"But Lyman has been real worried. He's tried not to let it show, but I can tell."

Mitch expressed the male point of view. "It's only natural for a husband to worry about his wife, especially when she's going to have a baby."

Jessie added, "Has Lyman been concerned about the money for the hospital bill?"

She nodded, and another strand of baby-fine blond hair came loose from the rubber band at her nape. "He's got enough to worry about already with the crops and the feed bill for the livestock due and the mortgage on the farm."

"It's hard work being a farmer," observed Mitch as he went down on his haunches not far from the girl.

She bit her lip. "Lyman works all the time. He's exhausted. He's only twenty-three, and I'm afraid that he feels like an old man already."

A painful spasm contracted in the region of Jessie's heart. "I know," she said soothingly as she pulled up another kitchen chair and sat down beside the girl. "It must be hard on you, too, Becky Sue."

"It's my fault," came out of the blue.

"What is?"

Embarrassed, and refusing to even look at Mitch, she blurted out in a rush: "We weren't ready to start a family. I forgot to take my pills and—"

They were words of small comfort, but Jessie voiced them aloud all the same. "Accidents do happen."

Lord knows, they happened every day to women a lot more sophisticated than Becky Sue Stoots.

The young face softened, and in doing so became even younger in appearance. "We both want our baby."

Jessie sighed. Children raising children. But she said: "It's good that you do."

Clear candid eyes searched out and found hers; they did not falter. "I've done something I shouldn't have."

The moment of truth. Jessie's heart began to pick up speed. "Have you?"

A quick nod. "You must believe that I didn't mean any harm by it."

She reached for the pregnant girl's hand and held it in her own. "I believe you."

"I do, too," said Mitch positively.

A grateful smile was directed at both of them. Encouraged by their belief in her, Becky Sue continued. "I'm very good with a needle and thread."

"I would venture to say you're an expert," judged Jessie. "I have the quilt you made for my grandmother last winter. It's beautiful."

That opened up a wellspring of information. "I love quilting, needlework, knitting, crocheting, needle-point, embroidery, cross-stitch. Especially if I'm allowed to make up my own designs. I wanted to go to art school, you know?"

"No, I didn't know."

"I could have gotten a scholarship, according to my teacher in high school."

Jessie suddenly felt like weeping for the girl. Dreams gone astray, and only eighteen years old.

Mitch seemed doggedly determined to return to the matter at hand. "Before Jessie's grandmother died, I understand the three of you had discussed the idea of placing some of your crafts in local gift shops."

The pretty blonde related: "That's what I decided to try to do. I knew Jessie had a lot else on her mind at the time, so I took a few of my things around on my own."

It was the first Jessie had heard of it. "What happened?"

She shrugged her thin shoulders. "Nobody was much interested. Oh, a couple of stores told me to come back in a month or two, maybe they'd take something then, but I didn't have a month or two. I needed the money right away."

Jessie could imagine the courage it had taken—and the rejection Becky Sue must have suffered. Her heart went out the girl. "What did you do next?"

"I took one of my tea-dyed quilts to the antique mall in town—" the pregnant girl was obviously very proud of having thought of it on her own "—and they agreed to try to sell it on assignment."

"Consignment?"

"Yeah, consignment."

"Did it sell?"

Bright blue eyes gave Jessie her answer even before she was told: "The very first day."

That got their immediate attention. "Did they mark the quilt as if it were an antique?"

"Oh, no, that wouldn't be right. The sign on it said plain as day, Not Old."

Jessie certainly wasn't going to quibble over the ethics of the fine line between not old and new. The practice was common enough in antique shops and malls all around the country.

Mitch was the one to say, "You must have been excited to make your first sale."

The girl's face lit up. "I was thrilled. The baby quilt sold for eighty-five dollars and I got to keep half." A pout on the pretty little mouth came and went. "Splitting the money fifty-fifty may not sound fair to you two, but I wasn't paying rent on a booth, or anything. They were nice enough to display my crafts by the front counter."

"And you were just grateful to make the money," said Mitch kindly.

Becky Sue's response was enthusiastic. "They even asked for more to sell, so I took in a quilted wall hanging, a petit-point pillow and a crocheted baby shawl."

Jessie slipped in. "When did you get the idea to make the sampler?"

Becky Sue didn't hesitate to tell them everything. "The old-fashioned looking stuff seemed to sell the best, so they suggested I borrow designs from antique quilts and stitchery. It was easy enough to do." She frowned in concentration. "Then one day I saw this really neat sampler in the Hillocks' kitchen, and I knew I could make a copy."

"So you drew a sketch on a brown paper bag and then went home and stitched a sampler just like Elizabeth's."

"Except for that funny little 's' in one of the words," she confirmed. "I decided to skip that part."

Mitch's eyes narrowed. "Did they agree to sell the sampler at the antique mall?"

Her eyes evaded his. "No."

That wasn't what he'd apparently expected her to say. "No?"

The girl wet her lips with anticipation and drew in a deep breath. "This time he said the sampler was too good to sell here in town, that we'd get a lot more money for it if he sold it in a big city somewhere."

"I see," said Jessie noncommittally. She deliberately avoided looking at Mitch, but she could sense his alert interest.

"We did, too."

"How much more?" she probed carefully.

The very young voice also became very small. "My share was five hundred."

Jessie wanted to make sure she hadn't misunderstood. "He sold it for a thousand dollars?"

A nod.

"That's a lot of money, isn't it?"

A second nod.

She hated to have to say it. "Perhaps too much money for a reproduction of an antique sampler?"

Yet another nod.

In a gentle, understanding tone, Jessie asked, "Is that when you began to suspect that your copy had been sold to someone as an original?"

A tearful nod.

"And you didn't know what to do about it?"

Becky Sue burst out with all of her guilt-ridden transgressions. "Don't you see? I couldn't tell Lyman. He would be so disappointed in me, even though we needed the money desperately. Our bill at Popplewell's was getting bigger and bigger. I couldn't sleep at night just thinking about it." The tears flowed unchecked down her cheeks. She tried to brush them aside. "Besides, he made me promise not to tell anybody. Not a soul."

Both of their heads came up. Mitch repeated: "*He?*"

The girl's lips tightened.

"You mustn't protect him, Becky Sue," Jessie told her. "He used you, and whatever you may believe you don't owe him your loyalty."

"But I promised."

"I know you did." Jessie thought quickly. There was always more than one way to catch a thief. "I have an idea."

"You do?" Becky Sue sounded hopeful.

"I do. I'll say somebody's name, and you nod your head yes if I'm right, or shake it no if I'm wrong. That way you won't really be *telling* us, and you won't be breaking your promise. Okay?"

The girl caught the tip of her tongue between her teeth and said in a guarded voice, "Okay."

Jessie looked from Becky Sue to Mitch and back again. She took a deep breath. "Was the man David Fenner?"

For a moment Becky Sue Stoots sat there in the Hillocks' kitchen, frozen like a statue.

Then she nodded her head.

Chapter Fourteen

All The Way Home

"You weren't the least bit surprised to find out it was David Fenner, were you?" said Jessie as she and Mitch drove along the country road toward the Brick family farm.

He uttered a slightly self-satisfied: "Nope."

"What made you think David was behind the scam?"

Mitch took off his sunglasses, pursed his lips as though he were going to whistle, then blew at a speck or two of dust on the surface of the dark lenses. He slipped them back on before answering. "I think it was this morning when Seth mentioned New Jersey."

"New Jersey?"

"A little bell went off in my head. I remembered the first day we visited the antique mall. You said that Thesslong Fenner's nephew from New Jersey had inherited everything."

"That's right." She was justifiably impressed. "Do you have a photographic memory?"

He laughed as he assured her, "Lord, no. Maybe just a good memory for the odd fact or two. I've been telling you all along—it's a certain knack we journalists acquire after years of working in the field."

She gave him the same telling glance she had the first time he had tried to feed her that line.

"Honest," he said, and laughed again.

They rode in silence.

After several minutes of thoughtful consideration, Jessie heaved a great sigh and speculated aloud: "What in the world are we going to do about David Fenner?"

"*We* aren't going to do anything. *I* will take care of Mr. Fenner."

"You'll take care of Mr. Fenner?" She was taken aback by his reaction to the question, not at all certain that she liked the implication behind his words.

She couldn't see the expression in Mitch's eyes due to his dark glasses, but she was intensely aware of him as he stated unequivocally: "You don't have to worry about it. But I'll be damned if the guy is going to get off scot-free."

"Get off scot-free?"

"Well, I don't think we should take this to the police."

Jessie shot him a puzzled look.

"Believe me, Jessie, the police have better things to do than chase down and prosecute a small-time hustler out to make a few hundred bucks. The David Fenners of this world aren't worth bothering with, not when there are all kinds of lowlifes out there." He gave her a quick sideways glance. "And unless you want to involve both Becky Sue and the Hillocks, and have them testify in court—"

She was shaking her head at the very idea. "That's the last thing I want to do. It would put a black mark on the girl's reputation that she'd never live down."

"I'd venture to say that Becky Sue has already learned her lesson the hard way."

Jessie nodded in agreement. "I made Alice and Seth promise that this entire affair would go no further than the four of us. Virgil Marquart doesn't really understand what occurred, and he never has to. I want it to end here and now."

"It's not quite ended," he informed her.

"What do you mean?"

"I mean, I don't like bullies and I don't like men who use innocent women." He muttered under his breath, "I'd like to beat the hell out of David Fenner."

"Oh, Mitch, violence never solves anything. What good would it do for you to beat up David Fenner?"

"I'd feel better and he'd feel a whole lot worse," he surmised with a certain grim amusement.

She shook her head and said quietly, "You'll never learn, will you?"

"I hardly think that's the point. It's Fenner who has a whole lot to learn. For crying out loud, Jessie, the guy was using a poor pregnant girl to make a few bucks. It could have ruined her life."

She knew that. But physical violence never solved anything. She knew that, too. She believed it with all of her heart and mind and soul. She despaired that she and Mitch would never see eye to eye on the issue, that it would always somehow separate them.

It was some time before Mitch said in a different voice: "I couldn't help but notice that you wrote out a check."

Her posture was ramrod perfect as she sat in the seat beside him. "I was paying Seth for framing Elizabeth's sampler."

He looked at her askance. "And..."

"And?"

"Surely the cost of framing hasn't risen that drastically."

"All right. You may as well know. I bought the reproduction that Becky Sue made."

He reached across and gave her hand an appreciative squeeze. "You're a nice lady, Jessamyn Jordan."

She felt the color rising in her face. "Anyone with a decent bone in their body would have done the same thing."

He crooked a rakish brow at her. "Well, I can vouch for that fact."

"What fact?"

"That you've got a decent bone or two in your body," Mitch drawled suggestively. "What are you going to do with the copy?"

She threw her loose chestnut hair back from her shoulders. "I haven't decided yet. Perhaps I'll have it temporarily removed from its frame—just long enough for Becky Sue to add her signature and the date where everyone can see it."

"And what do you have, but a fine reproduction by a local artisan."

"Precisely. Then I may donate this particularly fine reproduction, commissioned by my grandmother and myself, to the city hall or the library or some other deserving public institution. The girl really does have talent and I'd hate to see it go to waste."

Mitch's voice measured out controlled calmness. "Besides, one mistake shouldn't be held against her for the rest of her life."

"We all make mistakes."

"'To err is human'...."

"Exactly."

He turned onto the country lane that wound its way through the fields toward the Brick farm. "Unfortunately, some of us are apt to make a few more errors than others."

As he parked the Corvette in front of the house, Jessie said: "Thank you again for driving Becky Sue home, and then coming back to Hillocks' for me."

"It wasn't much, but you're welcome. Like I said, the poor kid deserves a break. She's just damned lucky you were the one who decided to give it to her."

"Anyone would have done the same."

His deep baritone was softly persuasive. "I don't think so, honey. You've got both a big bank balance and a big heart. In my experience the two rarely go hand in hand." His dark liquid eyes were filled with approval. "You've turned out to be quite a woman. Your grandmother would be proud of you."

Her lip quivered. "That's the nicest thing you've ever said to me."

"I mean it."

The sound of another car coming down the gravel road caught their attention. It was a dusty station wagon that purported to be dark blue, but gave the appearance of dingy gray.

"That must be Esther," said Jessie. "She mentioned something to me yesterday about coming over to work in the garden, or clean the parlor."

"She'll look after you as she looked after Christine."

"It's rather nice to know that someone is looking out for you."

He seemed vaguely preoccupied. "Yeah, it must be."

Jessie opened the passenger door of the Corvette and stepped out. It was a moment or two before she noticed that Mitch hadn't followed suit. "Aren't you coming in?"

He brushed the question aside. "Not right now. I've got some business to take care of."

She suddenly had an odd, unpleasant feeling in the pit of her stomach, but she forced herself to smile at him and inquire: "Will you be home for dinner?"

Evidently his mind was on something besides food. "You and Esther had better go ahead and eat without me. I don't know how late I'll be."

Jessie's heart sank. "All right."

"I'll give you a call later," he said, almost as an afterthought.

She watched as Mitch put the sports car into reverse, backed around and drove away.

He didn't bother to wave.

She was still standing there long after the dust had settled again on the country road.

JESSIE CURLED UP in the overstuffed armchair in the front parlor—one of the few genuinely comfortable pieces of furniture in the entire house—and opened her great-great-great-grandmother's journal.

At her insistence Esther Huckelby had gone on home after they'd shared a simple supper of fresh garden vegetables lightly steamed and buttered. A slice of peach pie, à la mode, had followed. They'd put most of the pie back in the pantry, saving it for Mitch.

It was nine o'clock and he hadn't called yet. It wasn't like him not to let her know when he was coming home. But Jessie reminded herself that the man didn't owe her any explanations for what he chose to do with his time. No promises had been made. No promises, therefore, could be broken. He was free to come and go as he pleased, she argued logically.

But her heart told her otherwise.

She thought back to the first occasion she'd had to visit his house: that great, empty, cold, cavernous house. The very sight of it had broken her heart. It was a house, not a home.

Later that same day, when he had brought her back to this house, this home, this place of her ancestors that she loved more than any other place on God's earth, she had stepped out of his car and implored him: "Please don't break my heart again."

She hadn't understood at the time why she'd said it. She still didn't. Except on some intuitive level she knew Mitch had broken her heart before, and that he was very likely to do so again.

Was she destined to fall in love with the wrong kind of man, just as Elizabeth had?

Why did she, as a Quaker woman, cherish peace while Mitch seemed to almost enjoy physical violence?

They were so different.

Were they *too* different? Was there any hope for them? Any future?

Jessie put her head back against the chair and closed her eyes. The tears flowed unheeded.

JESSIE AWOKE with a start and sat straight up in the armchair. Her heart was pounding in her chest and her skin was strangely damp with perspiration. Her breath was coming hard and fast, as if she'd been running. Her whole body was trembling.

She arose from the chair and stood in front of the parlor window and looked out at the night. Darkness had fallen while she'd dozed. The chime of the grand-father clock in the hall told her it was half-past nine.

There was a breeze coming in through the lace cur-tains. The perspiration dried on her skin. She felt a chill. She reached for the afghan kept year-round on the back of the horsehair sofa and pulled it about her shoulders.

How strange to be so cold on such a pleasant sum-mer night.

Her next thought did little to warm her: What had awakened her? She couldn't seem to remember.

Had she been dreaming?

Yes, perhaps it had been a dream. Then a second possibility occurred to her. Perhaps it had been an-other nightmare.

Suddenly Jessie sensed that something was wrong. Terribly wrong. It was Mitch. She knew it. She was sure of it. She could *feel* it. He was in trouble.

She wrung her hands in agitation. Dear God in heaven, what was she to do?

She threw off the afghan and raced into the kitchen for her handbag and car keys. One thing was for cer-tain. She wasn't going to sit idly by while something happened to him.

Their conversation in his car that afternoon came back to haunt her.

"*What in the world are we going to do about David Fenner?*" she had said.

"*We aren't going to do anything. I will take care of Mr. Fenner.*"

"*You'll take care of Mr. Fenner?*"

"*You don't have to worry about it. But I'll be damned if the guy is going to get off scot-free.*"

The words echoed in her head again and again: *"I'll be damned if the guy is going to get off scot-free. I will take care of Mr. Fenner."*

That's what she was afraid of.

Jessie squeezed her eyes tightly shut and whispered into the darkness: "I love you, Mitch. Please know that I love you. And I'm coming. I'm coming."

MITCH REACHED OUT his hand to try the front door of Fenner's and then hesitated. Just for an instant the image of Jessie's face flashed into his mind. It was the darnedest thing. He shook off the feeling and turned the knob.

It was unlocked.

He opened the door and walked into the restored Victorian mansion that served as the antique mall. The clock on the wall above the cash register read nine-thirty. It was after official business hours but there was still a light on in the office, and he could see David Fenner's blond head bent over a stack of receipts as he sat at his desk.

Without a sound Mitch made his way across the wooden floor. For a big man he'd always had the ability to move gracefully, quietly, silently. Like a jungle cat, some claimed. It had held him in good stead throughout the years: in his old neighborhood back in Coaltown, P.A., in the navy, in the boxing ring, once on a back street in Manila, another time in an obscure bar on an equally obscure South Sea island.

He struck a deliberately casual pose in the doorway of the office: leaning against the jamb, a toothpick stuck nonchalantly in one corner of his mouth.

He had been standing like that for a good minute, maybe two, before he spoke. "Evening, Fenner."

The man jumped. He started to get to his feet, and then apparently thought better of it. Instead, he sat back in his desk chair.

Mitch added: "Nice evening."

"Yes, nice evening. Mitchell Jade, isn't it?"

The guy knew how to keep his cool; Mitch had to give him credit for that. Of course, David Fenner also knew well and good who he was. The overly polite attitude, the I-can't-quite-remember-your-name-but-I-know-your-face-from-somewhere ploy was meant to rub it in just that much more. These Ivy-League types were all the same.

Mitch plucked the toothpick from his mouth and tossed it to the floor; it landed on David Fenner's handwoven, antique Persian carpet.

The man deigned to give him a second glance. Barely. "As you can see, Mitch, I'm rather busy right now. It is after our regular business hours."

He made a production of looking down at the watch on his wrist. "So it is."

The expression on David Fenner's features was studied; it bore traces of what the French liked to call "ennui." He affected a sigh and inquired: "What can I do for you?"

"Now that is a good question—what can you do for me?" he repeated with what must have sounded suspiciously like a threat. Mitch straightened, and they both recognized that the threat was real. "I'll tell you what you can do for me, Fenner. You can pack your bags and get out of town. Tonight."

The color drained from the man's face. All of a sudden his skin was the same pale, washed-out shade of blonde as his salon-styled hair. Still, he made a very good show of acting the injured party.

"Pack my bags? Get out of town tonight?" He laughed and rose to his feet. "You've got to be joking."

A muscle in Mitch's face started to twitch. That should have been a warning to the young Fenner, but he was too busy lighting a cigarette to notice.

"I never joke," Mitch informed him.

Fenner exhaled a billow of smoke. "Somehow I don't doubt that for a minute," he said disdainfully.

"You're leaving town."

Fenner sauntered past him and out of the office, casually tossing over one shoulder, "Well, I was thinking of a week on Bimini, but I really had January more in mind as the ideal time to vacation in the Bahamas."

Mitch pivoted on one foot. "You can start your vacation a little early."

The younger man stopped in the middle of what had once been the grand foyer, and turned to face his opponent. "Why would I want to do that?"

"For your health." There was no mistaking the implication.

"That sounds like a threat."

"It *is* a threat."

"I could call the police."

"You could."

A blond brow arched with curiosity. "But you don't believe that I will, do you?"

Mitch shrugged. "It's hard to say. You might. It's possible that you're even dumber than I think you are."

David Fenner's face reddened slightly.

"Go ahead. Pick up the telephone. There's one right behind you on the counter. Call the police."

Instead, the blond raised the cigarette to his mouth and took a long drag on it. He blew the smoke out from between his lips in a slow, steady stream. "You seem real anxious for me to do just that. Of course I have to wonder why."

Mitch baited him. "Yes, you do."

He affected boredom with the subject. "I suppose you will eventually get around to telling me."

"Eventually."

There was disrespect in the cultured voice when David Fenner said, "You really are a hoodlum, aren't you?"

Mitch laughed mirthlessly. "Now that's a word I haven't heard in ten, maybe even fifteen years."

"The police—?" prompted the other man when the conversation failed to continue.

"Ah, yes, the police. Personally I think they'll find the story of a certain fake antique sampler of great interest, don't you?"

"I haven't the slightest idea what you're talking about."

"I have a witness who says otherwise. And I have *both* samplers."

"You son of a—"

Mitch scolded, "Tsk-tsk."

"How in the hell did you find out about the sampler?"

He made a point of holding up one hand and casually examining each nail in turn. "I have my ways."

Fenner bit off a short expletive. "It was probably that naive little farmer's wife who squealed on me."

Mitch's voice vibrated slightly. "I'm afraid I don't know who you're talking about."

"Never mind." David Fenner's handsome blond looks suddenly deteriorated into what could only be described as true ugliness. "Maybe it was your girlfriend who figured out what was going on. I was concerned about that once I heard Jessamyn Jordan, antiques expert, was back in town." He gave a crude laugh. "You let me down, professor. I was counting on you keeping her so busy in the bedroom that she wouldn't have time to notice what I was up to around here."

Mitch's eyes became two pieces of stone. "You leave Jessie out of this."

"Maybe the rumor's true that you're planning on leaving town yourself. Maybe I won't have to, then. Maybe I'll stick around and comfort poor Jessie and her broken heart."

He refused to give the other man the satisfaction of knowing how close to the bone that one had cut. But he wouldn't—and he couldn't—let the insult pass. "If you even so much as look at Jessie wrong, I promise I'll break every bone in your puny little body."

Apparently that was the last straw.

The young Fenner threw his cigarette down and lunged at Mitch.

Mitch brought his own anger under control and simply stepped to one side.

David Fenner had the advantage of being five years younger, but he was also slower and a whole lot softer. He went sprawling, hitting the floor with a resounding thud, followed by the sound of tearing cloth.

Even with the sleeve of his designer dress-shirt half-torn from his arm and a trickle of blood dripping from the side of his mouth, the man came back for more.

"You won't think you're so tough once I beat the living daylights out of you, Jade," he vowed. "I don't think I've ever told you that I have a brown belt in—" He mentioned some exotic form of self-defense.

"Nope, you never did," admitted Mitch as he blocked a kick meant for somewhere in the region of his solar plexus. "And I don't believe that I've ever told you I was a boxer in the navy. Light heavyweight division. Fifteen knockouts."

That got David Fenner's attention.

Unfortunately for Mitch the next sound he heard was Jessie frantically calling out his name.

That got *his* attention.

He turned in the direction of her voice, and the young Fenner let him have it.

The floor rose up to meet him.

JESSIE HAD DRIVEN into town as if the devil himself was on her heels. Something, some instinct, some sixth sense, told her that she would find Mitch at Fenner's. The red Corvette parked outside the antique mall confirmed her worst fears.

Mitch had said he would take care of David Fenner. She only hoped and prayed that David Fenner wasn't "taking care" of Mitch, instead.

She parked her grandmother's Quaker-gray sedan and flew up the front steps of the building. The lights were on and the front door was unlocked. She turned the knob and stepped inside.

At that precise moment she saw David Fenner thrust his leg out in a vicious kick to Mitch's stomach, claiming he was some kind of karate expert.

They were fighting.

There seemed to be blood everywhere and sweat streaming down both of their faces; clothing was torn and bones very possibly broken. It made her physically ill just to think of it.

Dear God, they were trying to slaughter each other.

A cry of terror rose from her lips: "Mitch!"

He turned toward her, and that was when David Fenner chose to attack him from behind. Mitch went down like a ton of bricks, crumpling to the hardwood floor.

Her hand flew to her mouth and she watched in horror as the younger man advanced on his opponent. He intended to hit Mitch again while he was down.

She frantically searched for a weapon and found none. There was only a heavy antique brass lamp on a table at her elbow. It would have to do.

Jessie grabbed the lamp by its base, wielded it like a baseball bat, and with all her might rushed at David Fenner, ready to do whatever was necessary in order to save Mitch. "No! No, you will not harm him!"

She wavered only for an instant as she heard another voice echoing in her head: *No! No, thee will not harm him!*

The two battling men—both those in the present as well as those in the past—watched her, *had* watched her, as if they understood the choice she was forced to make was tearing her apart.

She thought her lungs would burst. She was certain her heart would shatter into a thousand tiny pieces. Her mind was on fire, her body as well. She was possessed of a superhuman strength beyond her wildest imaginings. But she was being torn, torn asunder, pulled in opposite directions by what she believed and what she must do. The dilemma was threatening her very soul.

She cried out in utter agony now as she had cried out then: *"Thee does not know what thee asks of me!"*

And in that single moment of time, with the past and the present as one, Jessamyn Jordan finally knew.

She knew that Elizabeth Banks had once stood thus, and—although it went against everything she believed in as a woman and as a Quaker—she had pulled the trigger and actually killed one man in order to save another.

Somehow she knew, too, that Major Nathaniel Currant had then taken the body of the dead marauder away and had buried it deep within the forest many miles from the Banks's homestead. The stranger's death had become their eternal secret: Elizabeth's and Nathaniel's.

Just as her great-great-great-grandmother before her, Jessie made the only choice she could.

She rushed toward David Fenner, screaming: "Touch him again and you're a dead man!"

He wasn't so easy to bluff. "I don't think so."

Another voice from behind Jessie said in a deadly tone, "Then you'd better think again."

It was Mitch, back on his feet and ready to fight.

David Fenner threw his hands up in front of him this time and backed off. "Hey, don't worry. I may be stupid but I'm not dumb. You can put the lamp down now, lady. I have no intentions of going one on one with your boyfriend."

But she didn't budge from her defensive stance until it was Mitch standing beside her, prying her fingers loose from around the base of the brass lamp as he assured her: "It's all right, sweetheart. You can let go now, Jessie. I've got everything under control."

She suddenly went limp with relief. Then she began to shake violently in reaction. Wrapping her arms around herself she tried to watch and listen and make sense of it all.

Mitch seemed intent on making the situation crystal clear to David Fenner. "You've got exactly one hour to get out of town. If you're still around after that, I'm calling the cops and letting them deal with you."

"What about the antique mall?" the younger man mumbled as he took a monogrammed handkerchief from his back pants pocket and held it to his mouth.

Completely devoid of sympathy for him, Mitch suggested, "I'm sure there's some deserving second or third cousin in town that would be happy to inherit the place. Somebody your uncle would have approved of."

Fenner glanced around the mall, then slowly made his way, limping, toward the door.

"You'd better get moving," Mitch called to him. "You've only got one hour, and the clock is ticking."

"I KNOW THE HOLY commandment that Elizabeth Banks could not forgive herself for breaking," Jessie was confiding to Mitch much later that night as she huddled beneath the afghan taken from the parlor and sipped a mug of black coffee she was pretty sure he had liberally laced with whiskey.

He sat across the kitchen table from her, holding an ice pack to the swelling bump on his head. "You do?"

She nodded. "I know it all now, you see."

"You know all of *what* now?"

"What happened the day the drunken marauders rode into the homestead."

Mitch sighed and seemed to blame himself. "You knew during the fight at the antique mall."

In a small, firm voice, she said, "Yes."

He seemed to understand well enough without her telling him. "It was the violence that brought back the memories, wasn't it? I could tell. I could see it in your eyes." He buried his head in his hands for a moment. When he looked up again, there was something terrible to behold written across his face. "I hope I never live long enough to see that look in your eyes again."

She shivered. "What look was that?"

"Fear. Fear and hate."

"No—" she protested.

"Yes," he insisted. "For one instant, there was no difference between me and the other man. We were both the enemy, and you felt nothing but fear and hatred at the sight of us."

She tried to explain to him again as she had in the past: "For the Quakers—the Society of Friends—the basic principles we have lived by for over three hundred years mean meeting violence with non-violence, hate with love, war with peace."

He looked at her thoughtfully.

"That's why we are pacifists, that is why during wartime our men and women often choose an alternate form of service to their country. We believe it's wrong to harm another human being. Violence only begets further violence. Anger, more anger. Hate, even greater hatred. To a Quaker woman, to a woman like Elizabeth Banks, even to a woman like myself, raising her hand in anger goes against everything she believes in."

"So the commandment Elizabeth broke wasn't 'Thou shalt not commit adultery'?"

Jessie acknowledged, "The commandment she couldn't forgive herself for breaking was 'Thou shalt not kill.'"

"'Thou shalt not kill.' Of course."

Facing Mitch, she related without anger, but with a kind of finality: "On that long-ago winter day, while her husband lay in bed with the Fever, Elizabeth Banks picked up his rifle and shot and killed the man named Maggot. She did so in order to save Nathaniel Currant's life. The act she committed—the murder of another human being—haunted her for the rest of her days."

"But she had no choice."

"She had no choice."

"If she hadn't shot him, Maggot might well have killed Nathaniel."

The truth of what he'd said was quietly accepted. "Maggot may well have killed Nathaniel, if she hadn't acted."

"But she still killed."

Jessie nodded. "She still killed."

"And you were prepared to do whatever was necessary tonight in order to save me."

"I was prepared to do whatever was necessary."

"Can you forgive yourself?"

"I don't know."

"Can you forgive me?"

"There's nothing to forgive in your case."

He studied her for a moment or two. "Then that's the real hell of it."

He was beginning to understand, it seemed.

"I admit I had hoped it would be different this time," she confessed. "I thought we could live in peace and harmony, in a world filled with nothing but love."

Mitch shook his head from side to side. "You aren't living in the real world, then, Jessie."

"Perhaps it's not real to you, but it is to me. I believe that such a world does exist."

He sighed and pushed his chair back from the table. "I was afraid it would come to this."

Her heart began to beat faster. "Come to what?"

He stood up and stared straight down into her soul. "I'm no good for a woman like you, Jessamyn Jordan. Hell, half the time I'm no damned good for myself."

Tears pooled in her eyes.

He continued. "I've tried to tell you that again and again. But you wouldn't listen."

"I heard you."

Mitch raked his fingers through his hair in a desperate gesture. "We need to talk, Jessie. Seriously talk." Then, almost as if he couldn't face the apprehension and wariness in her eyes, he averted his gaze. "But not tonight. Tonight you should just rest. You've had quite a shock."

Suddenly she was tired. Dead tired. She struggled to her feet and started toward the bed that awaited her upstairs. "What about you?"

She noted the scowl he tried to hide. "I'll be along in a while. I've got some thinking to do."

She swayed with dread. "Thinking to do?"

"I have a meeting with Richard Ratcliff and the university selection committee in the morning, remember? I'll be giving them my final answer at that time."

For a moment she failed to comprehend what he was saying. "Your final answer?"

When he turned to her his face was gray with fatigue and strain. "Whether I stay, or whether I go."

Jessie stood there in silence. Time had run out. She found that she had no words to make him stay.

SHE WATCHED from the second story window as Mitch drove away the next morning. For some reason she remembered a song that her grandmother used to sing to her when she was a child.

"But, Grandmama," she had always asked at the end of the melancholy tune, *"why are you crying?"*

"Because the words are sad, Jessie."

"Then why do you sing them?" came the child's question.

"Because the song makes me think of James," was Christine's standard answer.

"Grandfather?"

"Yes, your grandfather. There was a time during the Great War when I feared that I might never see him again."

"But you did see him again, Grandmama."

"Oh yes, my child. I not only saw him again, but I married him and we were given children, and grandchildren. We were given you."

"I'm glad you were given me, Grandmama."

"So am I, my dearest Jessamyn."

"Then why do you sing the sad song?"

"Because it reminds me that the only truly important thing in life is to love, to love one another."

Jessie hadn't really understood as a child. She did now.

She rested her head against the windowpane. She could almost hear the quiet alto of Grandmama's voice, so sweet and clear. The words of the old English folk tune—"Black is the Colour of My True Love's Hair"— ran through her mind and her heart.

As Jessie stood at the window of the Brick family farmhouse, she wondered.

Would she ever see her own true love again? Would Mitch come back to her?

She had no answers.

Chapter Fifteen

Home At Last

It was late afternoon on the same day and still Jessie waited and hoped, waited and hoped that Mitch would return.

She sat down in the familiar armchair in the front parlor and opened Elizabeth's diary for the last time. She read the final entries written in her great-great-great-grandmother's neat hand:

> April 2, 1822
>
> Now that Joshua is fully recovered, Nathaniel has decided to take a room at the boarding house in town. My husband did ask him to stay, but Major Currant did insist he must go. I do not know what we would have done without his help through this long and dreary first winter.

> April 18, 1822
>
> Nathaniel came to the Homestead today but he did not speak to me. I did see him atop the hill behind the cabin. He appeared to be planting a tree of some great variety. My husband informed me that the tree is called a Golden Raintree. I have never

before heard of this kind.

May 1, 1822

Major Currant did ride into our Homestead on this
day to bid us farewell. He has decided to go on
West. He says it has become too crowded here in
the County to suit him.

Joshua did make him a gift in parting. I did not
know until later that my husband had taken my
portrait down from our wall and, rolling it up, bestowed it upon Nathaniel.

I did give him my own parting gift. A wild rose
I had pressed between the pages of my Bible last
summer. Then Joshua and I did watch until our
friend rode out of sight.

July 20, 1823

It is more than a year now since Major Currant has
quit Henry County. We had one letter from him
last September. He was in the wilderness territory
and planning to keep on Westward. We have had
no other word from him since.

The Golden Raintree atop the hill is in bloom. If
thee stand beneath the branches and give them a
mighty shake, tiny yellow flowers do fall upon thy
face. It is a most wondrous thing.

August 29, 1823

Tonight after supper I did stand at our cabin door
and look across the green, green valley. I could see
the blue mist on this summer's eve as it drifted toward me. For the first time since I began to sus-

pect I am with child, I can feel new life within me. My heart has ceased to yearn for what it cannot have. This is our home now, Joshua's and mine. This is our Indiana home.

Jessie Jordan closed the antique leather-bound journal and rose to her feet. She walked out of the parlor and up the stairs to the second story of the old farmhouse, but she did not stop there. Opening the door to the attic, she climbed the narrow flight of steps.

In the large, dusty room she looked around at the myriad objects. There had always been something special, something wonderful about this place. Late-afternoon sunlight was flooding in through the row of west-facing windows on one end of the house, giving a warm glow, a golden patina, to the entire attic and its contents.

She walked toward an old Saratoga-style trunk in one corner and went down on her knees beside it. She slowly opened the lid. With great reverence she moved aside the beautifully kept baby clothes and placed Elizabeth Banks's diary at the bottom of the trunk. Then she closed it again and stood. It was not until that moment that Jessie realized tears had been streaming down her face all the while.

In another time and yet in this place, years hence, it was possible that another woman would discover the journal of her ancestor, and it would change her life as it had Jessie's. But that was not for her to say.

As for herself, perhaps, like Elizabeth she had seen the last of the man she loved. Elizabeth had watched as Nathaniel mounted his horse and rode away, never to know what happened to him, or where he had gone.

Had Nathaniel ever married? Had children? Had he been happy? Had he been loved?

Dear God, how had Elizabeth borne such sadness?

She could not bear the thought of never seeing Mitch again, of not knowing where he was, if he was happy, if he was well or even alive.

What if he didn't come back to her? How would she bear such a terrible burden?

In the silence of that time and place Grandmama's words came to Jessie: "I managed because I had to. As women have always had to. As you will."

And Jessie knew that somehow she would.

She walked back down the attic steps, leaving the past behind her, and hoping, praying, that she had a future.

MITCH SHOOK HANDS with first one and then another of the university selection committee.

"Congratulations, Professor."

"We're pleased by your decision, Jade."

"It's an honor to have you join our faculty," came a third comment as they filed past him and out of the conference room.

Richard Ratcliff was the last to come up to him. His face was beaming with pleasure. He pumped Mitch's hand up and down several times. "Mitch, I couldn't be happier."

He found himself grinning from ear to ear. "Thanks, neither could I."

"I must confess you had us on tenterhooks for a while. Even I wasn't certain what your answer was going to be to our offer," the older man ventured.

"You weren't the only one," he admitted.

"Jessie must be even more pleased than your colleagues are today."

Mitch ran a hand through his thick black hair in a typically nervous gesture. "I hope she will be."

A distinguished slate-gray brow arched in his direction. "You mean you haven't told her yet?"

"Not yet."

"Well, don't let me keep you any longer, then. You'll be wanting to get home to tell her."

Home.

Mitch furrowed his forehead in thought. "Yes, I will, won't I?"

Once they were outside he paused and gazed around the idyllic campus setting with its ivy-covered buildings, rolling green lawns and vast natural canopy of trees overhead.

"You were right about this place."

Richard smiled at him. "Of course, I was."

He turned his face up to the afternoon sun. "I think I'm going to like living here."

His colleague clapped him on the shoulder in a friendly parting. "Like I said before, I've lived in this part of Indiana all of my life."

"I haven't," admitted Mitch, "but it's still become home to me."

Home.

Such a plain, simple word to have so many meanings for so many people, he reflected as he climbed into his sports car and headed for New Castle and the Brick family farm.

Home.

He no longer thought of the small dilapidated house on West Berry Street as he had for years, nor of the people who had lived there. When he thought of home now he saw visions of cornfields and a neat row of red barns, the Happy Valley in the distance and a house full of love.

He thought of Christine and Elizabeth, and of all the woman before and after them.

But mostly he thought of Jessie. Jessie with her windblown chestnut hair and her long legs and her sweet loving ways.

He had changed.

He wasn't the same man he had been when he'd first come to this place eight short months ago. Then he would have described himself as a tired, cynical, world-weary journalist who was convinced that there were far worse things than being lonely and alone.

Now he couldn't imagine a day without Jessie in it.

He had once told her that being brave meant overcoming her fears. He was very good at giving advice to others. Maybe it was time—past time—for him to take some of his own good advice.

What was he afraid of?

He had faced and survived pain, violence, even death, since he was a child. He had often stared fear in the face. He had been alone for as long as he could remember. He had been unloved and unwanted most of his life.

What was he really afraid of, then?

The answer echoed in his head: If Jessie knew him down to the last bitter dregs of his soul she wouldn't, couldn't love him.

He was afraid of loving her.

He was afraid of having her love him.

He was afraid of losing her.

He was a coward.

Yet, how could he possibly manage the rest of his life if she wasn't part of it?

Staying had to do with what was here and now. *Going* was all about what was out there. Well, he had seen enough of what was out there to know that Jessamyn Jordan was the best damned thing that had ever happened to him.

He wasn't perfect, but he did love her. No man would ever love her more. He had to have the courage to stay and fight for what was his.

This time he would do it right. This time he would stay and make it work. This time she would be his.

His inner war was over. He would let go of his anger and hatred. Perhaps love could overcome hate, after all. He would come home at last.

Mitch came to grips with the truth, however painful, as he drove south along State Road 3.

A half hour later he turned onto the country road that would take him home in time for tea.

JESSIE FINISHED drinking her tea, rinsed out her cup and placed it in the drain rack. But she knew she was only going through the motions. Her mind was somewhere else, with someone else, with Mitch.

Where was he? What was he doing?

She had been hoping and waiting so long for him to return. Too long. It seemed like forever. The day had dragged on interminably. The telephone had been silent. Only Esther had been by to see her, and even she had had better things to do than baby-sit a grown woman. Jessie had sent the housekeeper on her way with an understanding hug and an "I'll be just fine."

She wasn't fine. But there was nothing anyone could do.

At least it was a perfect July day. The skies were clear blue, and there was a slight breeze out of the northwest to keep the temperature and humidity from becoming uncomfortable. Earlier that afternoon, she had spent an hour, perhaps closer to two, bent over in the garden, pulling weeds.

Hard work.

But as Esther Huckelby—and her mama, Goldie, before her—always said: Hard work never hurt nobody.

Weeding a large vegetable garden was a great equalizer, in Jessie's book. It definitely separated the men from the boys, the women from the girls.

Her hair was still a little damp from her recent shower, so she took a rubber band from the kitchen drawer and pulled the whole thick mass up into a ponytail. She slipped her feet out of the summer sandals she was wearing and donned a pair of worn Reeboks she kept by the stove. Then she pushed open the screen door and walked out of the farmhouse.

She paused on the back stoop, considering where she might go, then decided to climb the hill to the Golden Raintree. The great tree stood silhouetted against the summer sky, its branches heavy with foliage and hundreds, thousands, of bright yellow flowers.

The middle of July, it was the season for the Golden Raintree to be in full bloom. It beckoned to her, as it had beckoned to generation after generation of women in her family, women who had lived and worked and died for this land.

Jessie began the trek across the barnyard, through the high meadow and up the hill. She reached the summit and stood there, looking out over the Happy Valley. Summer had dressed the earth in full costume: fields abounding with cow parsnip, tiger lilies—those small orange trumpets she loved best of all—cascading over every fence post, blue chicory sprouting up alongside the roadway, pink clover in the meadows, abuzz with nectar-gathering bees.

It was all hers now to care for and look after: the farmhouse, the great Golden Raintree, the family cemetery, the fields as far as the eye could see and the green valley beyond. This was the legacy passed on by her grandmother. This was the inheritance she would one day bestow upon her own daughter.

If she ever had a daughter....

THE HOUSE was empty.

He went from room to room, calling out her name: "Jessie? Jessie, where are you?"

There was no answer. No one was there. At every turn Mitch met only silence.

He spotted the teacup in the drain rack. Someone had been here. He tentatively touched the china pot on the counter; it was still warm. Someone had been here not long ago.

He opened the door of the refrigerator and helped himself to a large glass of Esther's homemade lemonade. He put his head back and drank it in a single great gulp. The lemonade went down so fast that it made his throat ache.

Then he felt a small breeze blowing on his face and noticed that the back door was ajar. He took off his suit jacket and tossed it across the back of a kitchen chair, rolled up the sleeves of his white dress shirt and stepped out onto the back stoop of the farmhouse. He paused and looked around.

There wasn't a soul in sight.

Only the barns and the fields, a tractor or two, a herd of cattle in the distance, the cluck of a chicken out by the coop. Then he looked again and saw the outline of a woman standing on the summit of the grass-covered hill behind the house.

A great sigh of relief went through him.

There she was. He should have known where she would be.

A MAN WALKED OUT of the back door of the farmhouse and stood there on the stoop, searching the horizon. He had black hair and was dressed in black summer slacks and a white dress shirt. He must have spotted her, for he slipped on a pair of dark glasses and started toward her, following the path she had taken across the yard and up the incline.

It was Mitch.

Her heart began to pound in a joyful cadence as he loped toward her in long, easy strides. She watched him, wanting him, adoring him, loving him.

She thought back to that April day in Popplewell's general store. She never forgot the first time she saw him. She never forgot the first words he said to her.

He had come up to her that day, and said: "Remember me?"

Of course, she hadn't. She had thought he was a stranger.

Mitch came up to her now. He stood awkwardly beside her and said, "I'm sorry I missed teatime. The meeting with the selection committee took longer than I expected."

"I see," she murmured, watching him out the corner of her eye. He was so familiar to her and yet still a stranger.

"Aren't you going to ask how it went?"

"How did it go?"

"Fine."

This wasn't getting them anywhere. She tried again. "What did you decide to do?"

There. Now it was out in the open. Now the sixty-four-thousand-dollar question had been asked aloud. All Mitch had to do was answer it.

He took off his sunglasses and faced her as if she were the judge, jury and executioner in one. "I told the university that I was accepting their offer."

Jessie couldn't seem to get her breath, let alone make some appropriate response.

Mitch misinterpreted her silence. "I know you may not be thrilled with that bit of news. I realize that we have a lot of problems between us that we aren't even close to solving. But I do love you, Jessie. You must know that. I'm willing to try. I'm willing to change. I'll become whatever it is you need in a man. I know I'm no damned good for you. I don't suppose I've ever been any good for you. I've seen so much violence and hate."

She couldn't get a word in edgewise.

"I want you to forgive yourself for what you think happened at the mall last night. You are not a violent woman. I will try not to be a violent man…" He seemed to finally run out of steam.

"I've been doing some thinking, too, Mitch. Thinking and hoping and praying that you would come back to me."

He appeared shocked.

"Don't you understand even yet? My life is no good without you. It never has been. It never will be." Tears were bright in her eyes. "Without you, there's nothing."

He was visibly stunned, but he reached out and brought her up against him, enfolding her in his embrace. "You love me that much?"

"I love you that much."

"But I don't understand."

"I don't always understand it myself, but in my heart I know it's true."

There was an intensity burning in his eyes that set her afire. "I don't know what I did to deserve you."

A small womanly smile appeared on her face. "I guess you just got lucky."

He gave a great relieved burst of laughter. "Lucky—at last."

"At long last," she concurred.

He was suddenly pensive. "I've waited a long time for you, haven't I?"

Jessie sighed with the first real contentment she had ever known. "Yes. And I've waited just as long for you."

Mitch slipped an arm around her shoulders, and they turned together and looked out at the valley below them, the farmhouse, the fields ripening with summer corn. There was wonderment in his voice as if he couldn't quite believe his good fortune, his incredible luck. "This will be our home."

"Yes, *our* home."

He seemed bemused. "One day all of this will belong to our children."

"And someday to our grandchildren," she said. "Down through the centuries and across the years—generation after generation."

She told him what she believed with all of her heart and all of her mind and all of her soul. "The past, the present, the future—they really are as one."

It suddenly seemed to occur to Mitch, and a smile broke out across his face. "Maybe we'll have a daughter—or two."

"Maybe we will."

"Would you like that?"

"Very much."

He turned to her and his eyes darkened to a deep shade of green. "Maybe one of our daughters will stand beneath the Golden Raintree on a day in July with the man she loves."

Jessie reached up and shook a limb of the great old tree. Butterfly-soft petals brushed her face and his. "Maybe she'll shake the branches until the yellow blossoms rain down on their faces."

"And they'll catch them in their outstretched hands," he said to her in the hushed, husky baritone she had come to love above all other sounds.

"Golden rain."

Mitch caught a handful of magic rain; a wisp of wind blew it away. "Golden rain."

Jessie was laughing and crying at the same time.

Mitch turned and gazed down at her now, love shining brightly in his eyes. There was that special smile on his face. "Remember me?"

She hadn't forgotten the first words he said to her—apparently neither had he.

Jessie smiled up at him, her heart in her hands. "I remember you. I always have. I always will."

"I love you, Jessie," he whispered. "For the rest of my life and beyond."

Then they joined hands and walked down the hill toward home.

HARLEQUIN
Season's Greetings

Christmas cards from relatives and friends
wishing you love and happiness. Twinkling lights
in the nighttime sky. Christmas—the time for
magic, dreams...and possibly destiny?

Harlequin American Romance brings you
SEASON'S GREETINGS. When a magical, red-
cheeked, white-haired postman delivers long-lost
letters, the lives of four unsuspecting couples will
change forever.

Don't miss the chance to experience the magic of
Christmas with these special books, coming to
you from American Romance in December.

> #417 UNDER THE MISTLETOE
> by Rebecca Flanders
> #418 CHRISTMAS IN TOYLAND
> by Julie Kistler
> #419 AN ANGEL IN TIME
> by Stella Cameron
> #420 FOR AULD LANG SYNE
> by Pamela Browning

Christmas—the season when wishes *do* come true....

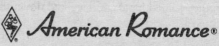

American Romance ®

Harlequin

HISTORICAL

CHRISTMAS

STORIES · 1991

Bring back heartwarming memories of Christmas past
with HISTORICAL CHRISTMAS STORIES 1991,
a collection of romantic stories
by three popular authors.
The perfect Christmas gift!

Don't miss these heartwarming stories,
available in November
wherever Harlequin books are sold:

CHRISTMAS YET TO COME
by Lynda Trent
A SEASON OF JOY
by Caryn Cameron
FORTUNE'S GIFT
by DeLoras Scott

**Best Wishes and Season's Greetings
from Harlequin!**

HARLEQUIN
American Romance®

COMING NEXT MONTH

SEASON'S GREETINGS

When a red-cheeked, white-haired mailman delivers four long-lost letters, four unsuspecting couples find that, at Christmas, wishes *do* come true!

#417 UNDER THE MISTLETOE by Rebecca Flanders

For Bret Underwood, nothing in the Currier & Ives town of Clayville, Indiana, had changed—except his best friend, Dani. Bret had spent a lifetime stringing lights across Main Street, but somehow this year, with Dani, was different. Would this be the year he got everything he wanted for Christmas?

#418 CHRISTMAS IN TOYLAND by Julie Kistler

Kristina Castleberry was a Scrooge—but this Christmas season a miracle happened and she magically found herself caught in a world of make-believe. When she met Tucker Bennett, Kristina made a secret wish. It was a big wish, but the most marvelous thing about Christmas is that Santa makes wishes come true.

#419 AN ANGEL IN TIME by Stella Cameron

Hannah Bradshaw had never believed in miracles until she was drawn back home to Georgia—and Harmony House, the magical place of years gone by. For as she thought of Roman Hunter, the young man she'd once loved, he appeared as though unchanged by time. What other surprises were in store for Hannah in this season of miracles?

#420 FOR AULD LANG SYNE by Pamela Browning

When an unexpected guest joined the gala Christmas Eve wedding festivities of her daughter, Leigh Cathcart began to believe in Christmas magic. But the presence of Ross Thornton, her college sweetheart, became unsettling when Leigh felt threatened that he would discover the secret she'd been guarding for twenty years.